YARETZI

Kanika Marwah

Ukiyoto Publishing

All global publishing rights are held by

Ukiyoto Publishing

Published in 2020

Content Copyright © **Kanika Marwah**
Cover Design & Illustrations Copyright ©
Mandy Khumanthem
ISBN 9789357870252

All rights reserved.
No part of this publication may be reproduced, transmitted, or stored in a retrieval system, in any form by any means, electronic, mechanical, photocopying, recording or otherwise, without the prior permission of the publisher.

The moral rights of the author have been asserted.

This is a work of fiction. Names, characters, businesses, places, events, locales, and incidents are either the products of the author's imagination or used in a fictitious manner. Any resemblance to actual persons, living or dead, or actual events is purely coincidental.

This book is sold subject to the condition that it shall not by way of trade or otherwise, be lent, resold, hired out or otherwise circulated, without the publisher's prior consent, in any form of binding or cover other than that in which it is published.

To the love that *is* us

Acknowledgements

To, Nanaji, Nani and Daddy: I love you.

To, Mummy, Papa, Garima, Manu: Thank you for giving me the freedom to be myself.

To, Sushma, Thoinu and Surbhi: Thank you for being my strength when I didn't have any.

To, Teyangsen: Thank you for walking with me.

To, Archana and Mayank: Thank you for the joy that you bring in my world.

To, Mandy: Thank you for all that you brought to this story.

To, Team Ukiyoto: Thank you for your incredible part in this journey.

To, the Universe: I do believe in magic.

And, to myself: Thank you. Couldn't have done it without you.

CONTENTS

One: The Introduction	1
Two: Monsieur Soleil	5
Three: Bougainvillea	8
Four: The Poster	11
Five: The land of Iris	17
Six: The question	21
Seven: The evening of October twenty-ninth	26
Eight: The first day of School	36
Nine: Back in room	42
Ten: The after	47
Eleven: The Meet	52
Twelve: The story of Acorns	57
Thirteen: Looking Around	59
Fourteen: The oldest boy	63
Fifteen: The Beams	65
Sixteen: An Impact	71
Seventeen: The Yellow Beam	76
Eighteen: The Layers	83
Nineteen: The Name	87
Twenty: The Waterfall	93
Twenty-One: Loved ones	99

Twenty-Two: The Second Tenet	106
Twenty-Three: Sponges	117
Twenty-Four: A conversation	123
Twenty-Five: The Revelation	132
Twenty-Six: The Light Beings	137
Twenty-Seven: Behind the Scenes	142
Twenty-Eight: The Bravest Thing	153
Twenty-Nine: The Final One	158
About the Author	163

One: The Introduction

There was a bright glow of light. Almost like sunlight pouring through a dark day. She felt the bright pierce of light on her body. It made it hard for her to open her eyes.

At the same time, she saw herself lying on the bed. It was like being able to observe herself from the outside. A heightened awareness of sorts. A miracle. Or a dream?

It was then that she saw those five sparkles hovering over her sleepy body. The sparkles were a mix of five different colors and her body was immersed in their collective light.

And then the alarm rang, and she woke up. It was six in the morning and on time, like always, Eiva entered her room.

***

2 | *Yaretzi*

Yaretzi is thirteen years old. And this is the month of October as we are recounting the story. The girl that we saw lying on the bed - with long black hair and bright blue eyes is her, our own hero of the story.

She has round cheeks and an even rounder body, and a serious love for the blue woolen pajamas that she is wearing this morning.

The woman who entered her room just a moment ago, was her mother - Eiva Loret.

Eiva and Yaretzi are almost equally tall with the mother being just a few inches taller. Eiva has short black hair that almost reach her shoulders. They're mostly straight and well-trimmed. Yaretzi's hair, on the other hand, are usually found ruffled and messy.

The exchange of the morning kiss and greetings later, she picked her body off the bed and shuffled her feet to the washroom. Winter mornings make her groggy, and so does the idea of going to school. Not an inherent trait - just something she picked up a few months ago.

As she stood before the washroom mirror, Yaretzi tucked in her stomach and held her breath - just to see if she looked better with her stomach in. Did she? She can't decide.

Maybe, she looked the same either way. Weird and uninteresting. Not a popular choice to befriend.

Some thirty minutes later, there is a knock on the washroom door. "Are you done, sweetie?" It's David - Yaretzi's dad. He's wearing grey track pants this morning and his favorite black hoodie. The track pants make his (already long) legs appear even longer. And the white framed glasses give him a solid look. At least, that's what he believes.

As Yaretzi stepped out of the washroom, David sat her down to make her hair. This morning he decided to do something different. He took her long hair and carefully propped them on to the sides of her face. It gave Yaretzi an appearance of having two giant black circular ears.

They agreed to go downstairs like that, and Eiva almost gasped.

"OH BOY DAVID! What is THAT?"

She gave the father and daughter a stern look, before hitting her husband on the shoulder. "You'll get her late for school. Come on, put her hair back in place while I get the breakfast ready." "And you," she said to Yaretzi, "stop teaming up with your dad."

They laughed together, hearing the last obligatory request and before the hot chocolate and spinach quiche reached the breakfast table, the hair was thankfully put in place and several looks of mischief exchanged between the father and daughter.

Not teaming up was not an option.

Two: Monsieur Soleil

David, Yaretzi and Eiva live in the land of Iris. They moved here in July this year. Before that, they had lived in Bougainvillea - the three of them along with Monsieur Soleil Maxil, Yaretzi's grandfather.

M. Soleil passed away two years ago, on a cold winter morning. Yaretzi was in her room sleeping when she had heard those voices coming from the outside. She had turned to look at her alarm clock. It was still early. Just five in the morning.

She wished to sleep some more, but something inside had told her to go check what was happening. Barefoot and sleepy-eyed, she stepped out of her room, and the next set of events unfurled rather quickly.

A group of three men - one of them being David - were carrying her grandfather's body out through the front door.

6 | *Yaretzi*

All Yaretzi remembers of that image is her grandfather's arm dangling from the side. Limp and lifeless.

She rushed downstairs then and had just reached the front door when she caught the final glimpses of an ambulance hurriedly drive away.

She spotted her mother standing next to the white bamboo fence. Eiva's arms were folded and there was anxiety all over her face.

She ran towards her and tucked at her shawl. They had found Opa unconscious in his room, her mother said. Just a few minutes later, Yaretzi learned about her grandfather suffering a cardiac arrest.

Monsieur Soleil had just been admitted for an hour when he passed away.

It was in that morning that Yaretzi experienced the fear of losing a loved one, and then moments later, the actual grief.

She had never thought she'd lose her grandfather. Like he was something that could be lost. It just didn't seem possible. Even the idea seemed bizarre. It hadn't existed in her world. It hadn't, until then.

Maybe, she'd thought he'd always be there. Only, she didn't know that always too had an ending.

Yaretzi didn't get to meet him. Didn't get to say her goodbye. And just like that a chapter had ended, and so had a beginning.

Three: Bougainvillea

An autumn scene from Bougainvillea

Bougainvillea is a small town amidst the hills. An array of plant and bird species is a staple there.

But the highlight is the pink flowering plant with which the town shares its name. Bougainvillea. Its fallen petals can be found all over the footpath - all through autumn to spring.

Each morning as the sun rises from behind the hills, the lazy chatter of the vendors, and the bubbling laughter of children walking to school fill the streets.

In the middle of Bougainvillea is a lake. A beautiful blue one that glistens when sunlight pours over it. It is home to several ducks and swans, who are now a part of Yaretzi's favorite memory.

Many evenings, as the sun had been about to set, Yaretzi had walked over to the lake with her grandfather. All the while holding his hand.

There, as Monsieur Soleil sat on the bench, she fed the birds shredded lettuce and peas. Sometimes, M. Soleil bent over and fed the birds too, even on days when his legs were aching.

Yaretzi used to enjoy looking at the white swans and their excited flutter of wings.

Even now, she dreams of those moments sometimes. Dreams feel like a wonder-filled realm because it is here that she even gets to meet M. Soleil at times.

His eyes are still as black, and his skin appears still as wrinkled. He smiles at her often in the dreams. His smile - that's another thing that hasn't changed. Everything else appears unreal.

Some mornings when she wakes up from these dreams, Yaretzi wishes to hug M. Soleil. To be cocooned in that warm embrace, once again.

What all would we do if we got to do them again? Just, once again.

Four: The Poster

The afternoon that Yaretzi received the poster was an ordinary day at school. The classes had started with Mr. Brian's lesson.

Mr. Brian is Yaretzi's Science teacher. He is partially bald and wears specs that are too large for his face. He is an ardent lover of books and likes to share his readings with the class.

Every now and then, he brings photocopied pages from some book that he'd enjoyed. That morning too, he had brought photocopied sheets and distributed them amongst all students to read.

The title had read, 'Stars: A brief study.'[1] The long paragraphs spoke the following:

Stars receive their brilliant light because of the energy released by the nuclear fusion reactions that

---

[1] *Stars: A brief study has been referred from* http://www.physics.org/article-questions.asp?id=52

occur at their cores. These are the very same reactions which created chemical elements like carbon or iron - the building blocks that make up the world around us.

Yaretzi had skimmed through the page to read the ending:

A supernova is a colorful explosion giving off brilliant light. It occurs when a massive star explodes at the end of its life. In this process, a great amount of energy releases.

Due to the explosion, different elements also get dispersed across the universe. This causes stardust to scatter - the same stardust which now makes up different planets including the Earth.

After reading, Yaretzi looked around the classroom. Almost all students were sitting clueless and confused - some scratching their heads even.

Mr. Brian stepped in front of the class and took his turn between different desks. He liked to build suspense in his lessons.

At last, he rubbed his hands and said, "Dear students, your reading for today reminds us that we are made of the same stuff as the stars."

He paused and reread the last paragraph, out loud.

Due to the explosion, different elements also get dispersed across the universe. This causes stardust to scatter - the same stardust which now makes up different planets including the Earth.

And then he added, "You, me, all of us - have stardust inside us."

He concluded there, and the bell rang, telling them that so had the lesson.

***

The rest of the day had gone on as usual for Yaretzi, until it was time for the lunch/break hour, or what they refer to at Blooming Springs as 'the recess.'

Well, how do we describe the recess hour at this school?

   A. There is a lot of chatter.

   B. There is a lot of running.

   C. There is a lot of shouting. It's MAYHEM!

14 | *Yaretzi*

As soon as the bell sounds, the kindergarten students rush out of their classrooms and head to the swings area. The older students prefer going to the soccer and cricket fields. Some students chose to stay back in classrooms, huddle in groups and have a cozy conversation over shared lunches.

Yaretzi, however, decides to spend this time differently. She picks up her tiffin box, notepad and a pack of colored pens, and heads straight to the swings area.

Just behind the twisted yellow slide and the orange see-saw is a clearing. It is made mostly of dry sand and small stones.

In its corner, however, stand two orange trees. Between them lies a patch of scattered grass - just where Yaretzi prefers to sit.

That afternoon, her tiffin contained mushroom and caramelized-shallot sandwiches. The sandwiches made her smile.

Some afternoons, as Yaretzi eats her lunch in the clearing, small white flowers fall in her lap. The wind brings them often.

She likes picking these flowers up and taking a sniff of their scent. The fragrance reminds her of a distinct land. As though she's known these flowers from way before. As though they are carrying a message. A remembrance.

After eating her lunch, she looked at the sunlit sky.

She thought she saw a bright glow. Almost purple in shade. She squinted her eyes, but then it was gone. Only the sun shone at her then.

She turned her face away and rested her head on her folded knees.

Some afternoons she doodles after having eaten. That day though, she thought away. How many places one could visit with thoughts alone!

And as she sat there with her thoughts, she made a silent wish.

She must have been there for quite a while because when she returned from her land of thoughts, the atmosphere had grown remarkably silent. The bell must have rung, and the students must've returned to the academic area.

She got up and hastily stuffed the pens and notepad back in her coat pocket. She'd just bent down to pick her tiffin box, when she saw that glossy white sheet of paper. The poster.

The spot in the clearing

Five: The land of Iris

The evening David, Eiva and Yaretzi moved to the land of Iris was in mid-July. It had rained for the entire five hours that they had travelled from Bougainvillea to this place.

Yaretzi was sitting with her side pressed to the window. Watching the million drops trail away.

At some point during the travel, she had also slept off. With a warm blanket covering her body. It had felt secure and warm in the car then. A cozy escape.

They had reached their new house around six in the evening, and Yaretzi wasn't sure if she wanted to step out of the car. She would have preferred being in Bougainvillea.

She still prefers it to the land of Iris. She'd choose it, any day.

This new city was so different. It didn't have Bougainvillea's hills or birds. It didn't have its flowers. It didn't even have the lake. The lake. How could a place not have a lake? It didn't feel like home without it.

This new city - the land of Iris, was situated on a plain. It seemed to have a big green cover. There were trees everywhere that Yaretzi looked. Huge trees and fresh grass. But they were still not the lake. Nothing could be like the lake.

A few weeks after their shift, Yaretzi's mum had shown a new fascination with photographs. She'd begun putting up framed photos along the staircase wall. White frames. Both her parents seemed to prefer white.

The photographs must be somewhere between fifty to a hundred. Yaretzi wasn't sure. She never counted them. She never even half stopped by to look at them.

Looking at the memories of the past, in the middle of all these changes, didn't seem so exciting.

The whole task had taken much time and efforts. But her mother had stuck by. Her dad had helped too.

By the end of it, the photos did seem to bring a sense of familiarity to the wall and the house. But even then, to Yaretzi, it didn't feel like her own.

There was something about Bougainvillea that could never be replaced.

When they were there, David and Eiva had run a small restaurant on the hillside. Work had been much which caused them to spend long hours at the restaurant.

While shifting to the land of Iris though, they'd decided to switch to a catering business.

Something that they could run from home. This gave them a lot more time with each other, but mostly with their daughter. After M. Soleil's passing, they didn't want her to be at home, alone.

In the early few months, while they were making this transition between the restaurant and catering, they ensured that one of them was home with Yaretzi, at all hours.

Just to be there for her, if she ever needed them, so that, she wasn't suddenly without anyone to lean on.

Yaretzi noticed this too. She notices a lot of things - most of which she doesn't talk about. She thinks she might worry the other person.

That's the thing about her - she thinks a lot. She doesn't want to worry her parents or anybody else.

And for the same reasons, she hadn't yet told anyone about the first day of school and everything it had contained.

Six: The question

For a month before receiving the poster, Yaretzi's mind was filled with ideas. Ideas about certain movies and books. To watch this movie and to read this book.

Some of their titles, Yaretzi had not even heard of before.

Maybe, she had unconsciously picked them up from somewhere.

For a few moments, she would resolve to go ahead with the idea. But, before she could pick up the book or find that movie, it would stop seeming interesting.

It wasn't so much about the idea anymore, she thought. It was about her. She didn't have the will in her to do many things. Much of life seemed uninteresting.

She didn't even realize when she'd become this way. She wasn't always like that, was she?

Once when she was in the library at school, a book had fallen over from a top shelf.

She had read its title. 'The Blue Flowers.' It seemed intriguing. Something that she could read. She thought of borrowing it with her library card and taking it home.

But then, halfway in her tracks, the idea started seeming too laborious. She couldn't go ahead with the whole thing.

There was this other thing about Yaretzi: more than her not wanting to do things, it seemed to her she couldn't do them. Like they would draw out a lot more from her than she could give. She didn't have the energy reserves for them anymore.

And so, the book went back to the shelf and the ideas probably back to where they had come from. Both waiting to be picked.

And so was her will.

***

That afternoon when she received the poster though, was different. Not to an extreme degree but, different.

When she saw the white glossy sheet of paper, it was lying on the ground. With its face down. At first, she looked around. Maybe, someone was playing a prank.

But when she saw no one, Yaretzi picked up the poster and turned it around. The poster informed her about a meteor shower.

'*On Saturday, October twenty-ninth, at twenty-two hours.*' It was the same day as she'd received the poster.

In usual circumstances, she would have left the poster just there. Lying as it was. But that day, she wanted to take it home. To show it to her parents. To go ahead with the whole thing. To watch the meteor shower.

Why it felt different to her, she didn't know. It didn't even feel so different while she was going ahead with it. While she was still in the process.

It was only in hindsight did she realize that that afternoon had indeed been different. Special even. Sometimes, we only know of them when we look at them later.

October twenty-ninth was a Saturday which meant they had clubs' meeting after school. Thus, she had to stay back for an extra two hours.

She reached home at about quarter to five and rushed straight into the living room.

Her parents were out due to some urgent business and a neighbor - an elderly lady of about seventy - was sitting on the living room sofa. It was the first time that Yaretzi was seeing this old lady.

Well, she had seen the lady before, but never inside her house. She didn't even know her name. What was this woman called?

The lady smiled at her. Yaretzi noticed that she had no teeth. She tried smiling back at the woman, but it came out awkward.

On hearing that it would take an hour for her parents to return, she rushed to her room upstairs and locked herself in.

She didn't want to go down and talk to the woman. She didn't want to be with her alone. Damn. She didn't know what to do. Why was she like that?

And just like that, Yaretzi slipped on her bedroom floor and began crying.

The tears and sobs came out heavy and rushed. It was as though even the crying was taking efforts. Why was she so scared of strangers?

Why couldn't she just talk and simply let herself be? That was the question. Why couldn't she just let herself be?

Seven: The evening of October twenty-ninth

The work took longer for Yaretzi's parents than expected, and they returned after seven. The old lady - Mrs. Pearl, was still sitting on the sofa when they got back.

She had made herself some tea to keep warm. The parents thanked her profusely and apologized for having made her wait.

The work was urgent, and they hadn't known whom else to ask. They hadn't even known that it would take so long. They were sorry.

The elderly neighbor just brushed her hand at them and said that they were worrying needlessly because she had had a great time.

She then gestured to let them know that their daughter was upstairs. She hadn't been able to go check up on her because of her knees.

But she wanted to. She wanted to know if Yaretzi was alright. David went upstairs at once. Eiva walked with the neighbor to the front door.

Before exiting, Mrs. Pearl held Eiva's hands and told her that she understood. That she understood well. And then offered her a smile to say that she hoped it would all be okay.

***

There was a loud knock on the door, and that's when Yaretzi woke up.

She was on the bed, clutching the white glossy sheet to her chest. She didn't realize when she'd fallen asleep. The knocks came again. She could hear her dad call out to her.

That evening her parents sat with her on the bed, for a long time. They held her close. Neither of them said much.

They got the dinner to her room and had it there on a laid mat.

Onion soup with spaghetti carbonara. That was a perk of having professional chefs for parents. The meals were always something to look forward to.

While having dinner, Yaretzi showed them the poster. The page was crumpled, but clear. David straightened it out and laid it between themselves.

Yaretzi wasn't sure if her parents would be interested in the idea. They seemed tired too. After the evening's breakdown, she herself didn't seem to have so much energy for a meteor shower.

The only thing that made her want to see it though, was that she'd never heard of a meteor shower. At least, not one happening in real life.

The only other time she'd heard of one was in a story M. Soleil had narrated to her long back. But that had been a story. She didn't know if meteor showers occurred commonly in real life.

"Meteor shower?" Eiva spoke up, "It sounds like a fancy rare event. Why did we not hear anything about it on the broadcast?"

David scratched his head. "Yea, I don't remember hearing anything about it either."

"When is it happening though?"

David looked at the poster again. "Tonight."

"What? Is it tonight? Wait let me see."

Eiva grabbed the poster and read it for herself.

"It's at twenty-two hours. That's 10pm. Shoot! We just have an hour until it starts."

"Yea. Shoot." And both her parents started laughing.

Yaretzi was still looking at them. At the crazy lot she got as parents. Did she choose them, or did they choose her? She would have to wait until the gap between two lifetimes to find out about that.

Even though she had had a crappy day, she felt good in their presence. That was another thing that hadn't changed. Being with her parents still made her smile.

Her dad was funny. He liked to make them laugh. She didn't know what made him laugh, though.

One night after moving to the land of Iris, she'd gone downstairs to get water for herself. She didn't even know what time it had been. Probably somewhere after twelve.

When she got down, she saw her dad sitting on the sofa. His shoulders were bent, and she could hear his sobs. A part of her wanted to go and hug him. That's what he would have done if they were in alternate positions.

But she couldn't make herself go to him.

Even later, she didn't mention that night to her father. Didn't bring it up with him. Didn't ask him what had gone wrong.

More than for herself, she was scared for him. Maybe, he wouldn't have wanted her to be there. She was scared to intervene. It just felt that that space belonged to him.

"Yaretzi?"

Her parents were looking at her now.

"We were asking if you want to watch it. The meteor shower?"

"Yea. I do." She said. "But, if you're tired, we can skip it. I mean I am sure it'll happen again. It could happen again, right?"

"It could." David thought with her.

"Whether or not it would happen again, we're watching it tonight." Eiva declared, and David nodded his head.

So, they were watching the meteor shower. It was decided.

They were amazing, her parents. That was true. She seldom told this to them. She hardly ever told this to her own self. David and Eiva were the stars of her galaxy.

Only if she could tell them. Only if Yaretzi could ever tell people how she felt about them.

They were out in the front lawn within an hour.

And so were blankets, shawls, cushions, and warm ginger-carrot cupcakes. Eiva had insisted on adding glazed almonds on the cupcakes. Final touches, she said.

David had set a mattress for them to sit on, and on his wife's demand, put a bonfire in place. The night was turning out to be more exciting than Yaretzi had thought it would be.

She had liked looking at stars even as a kid. She had liked it for as long as she could remember. That had been her favorite pastime with M. Soleil.

He had liked looking at stars too. They used to do a lot of things together while her parents were at the restaurant.

Besides watching the stars, solving sudoku puzzles was another one on their list.

M. Soleil had been a lover of Math. Stars and Math - did they even go together? He had enjoyed solving those puzzles.

One evening, when Yaretzi was probably seven or eight, she had sat with him to solve the puzzle, and she had solved it fast. Well, at least faster than her grandfather had.

He had been stunned. How could a child solve it so fast, when he took so much longer? He had wanted to know her tricks.

At first, Yaretzi didn't budge. Not because she didn't want to share her tricks but because she didn't know if she had any. She just solved sudoku the only way she knew. But M. Soleil kept insisting. He was certain a trick was involved.

Thus, that evening, as the sun descended behind the hills, Yaretzi sat with him in his study, and became his teacher. That was the first time she taught her grandfather something. And the first time that she learned how much he'd loved to learn.

***

"Why hasn't it started yet?" Eiva was peering intently at the sky.

"I don't know. It should have started by now. It's been more than ten minutes past ten, already."

"Did we get the time right?"

"Yea, I think we did. Where is the poster?"

"I don't know. I think we left it in Yaretzi's room. I went to the kitchen, and then came outside straightaway."

"Do you want me to get it?"

"I don't…"

"MUM. DAD. LOOK!" Yaretzi's excited voice interrupted their banter. She was pointing straight at the sky.

There was a shooting shimmer of silver. The atmosphere was quiet. Even the crickets had stopped chirping. They were looking at the sky, still. A shooting meteor came from deep under the right horizon. Another one shot immediately from the left sky.

And then one after another, bright glowing meteors filled the dark blue sky. Their blazing speed left trails of gas. It was like watching fireworks and many rockets - without any smoke or sound.

Where did these meteors come from? Yaretzi thought. Were they here to remind us of a faraway land?

Their eyes were glowing with the lights in the sky. And without even realizing, they had hugged each other closer.

Perhaps, a love for one thing births in us a love for another.

The Evening of Meteor Shower

Eight: The first day of School

It was July twenty-second, Yaretzi's first day of school. They had moved to the land of Iris only a week ago.

Yaretzi had wanted to stay home for another week. And another, if she could. The classes at her school though had started on July eleventh, and so to her parents, waiting longer didn't seem like such a good idea.

Her dad accompanied her to school that morning. She was quiet for most of the journey. Her dad was quiet too. Only the music played between them.

Upon finally reaching the school, David caressed her cheeks and said, "I hope you have an amazing day, but even if it's not so amazing, it'll be okay."

He kissed her. She got out of the car and went straight for the school building. Without looking back.

The first thing she noticed upon entering the school premises was the maroon board that read 'Welcome to Blooming Springs.'

The notice board told her that her classroom was on the second floor. So, she made her way towards the flight of steps, crossing giant potted plants that were put on the concrete path. She liked those plants. She liked all plants. At least, something was right.

The corridor on the second floor was a long rectangle, with four classrooms on either side. Yaretzi clutched the straps of her bag tighter as she moved her way across them.

Drawing in a sharp breath before entering the classroom, she repeated her father's words from the morning. It would all be okay. Inside the classroom, things indeed were alright.

Nobody seemed to have noticed her enter because they were all busy in their chatter.

Yaretzi didn't take notice of the number of students around her, or of what they were doing. What she looked for instead, was an empty desk where she could hide herself.

Lucky enough for her, she did find one. The corner seat of the last row. It was a relief that not everyone chose to sit on the back seats.

Immediately upon sitting down, she drew out the notepad and colored pens from her backpack and began to doodle.

Doodling was her escape. It took her to a different world. A world where she heard no other voice but her own. A world where she could just be. How easy everything would be if we all got to be ourselves. If we could all just be.

A singing good morning brought her back to the classroom. What? Really? Did they still sing it to greet it? The lady who had entered the class was wearing a knee length blue dress, and her hair was auburn. Wow. That was a pretty shade.

The teacher introduced herself as Ms. Smiths and looked at her for a fleeting moment before calling out the roll call.

Yaretzi nervously answered to her name. It was the last in the list. Shortly after, Ms. Smiths requested her to step in front of the class and introduce herself. All heads immediately turned around to look at her.

Their collective gaze caused her throat to run dry. She wasn't prepared for this. She didn't know how to introduce herself without wanting to run away. Literally.

The first thing she did upon reaching there was to clear her throat. She thought she'd cleared it a little too loud. Why did she have to do that?

She turned to look at Ms. Smiths. The teacher was smiling at her. Okay, so it was okay. Nobody noticed. She could go on.

"Hi. Umm, my name is Yaretzi."

"We can't hear her." Somebody from the last few rows said.

"Darling, can you speak a little louder?" The teacher stepped beside her and put her arms around her shoulders. That made Yaretzi more nervous. Why did a physical touch have an opposite effect?

She raised her voice this time. "Hi. My name is Yaretzi."

"Hi." The teacher said, stepping a little away this time. Phew! "Can you tell us a little bit more about yourself?"

Yaretzi wanted to say, 'there is nothing more to tell.' But instead told them about being new to the land of Iris.

"Oh really?" The teacher was thrilled. "Where did you live before this?"

"Bougainvillea."

"Bougainvillea!" Ms. Smiths clapped her hands. "What a pretty little town! I have always wanted to visit. How many members are there in your family, Yaretzi?"

"Four. No, three. Just my parents and I."

"I see. Do they both work?"

"Yes. They're chefs."

"That's lovely. Thank you. You may take your seat now."

That went okay. Didn't it?

Yaretzi had just entered the row of seats when she heard someone whisper. "Ugh. She's so fat. Who would even like to be her friend?" "Yea," her partner replied, "no wonder her parents are chefs." And then, there were giggles.

Yaretzi stopped for a moment before continuing to walk in. She didn't even turn to look at them. She didn't want anyone to notice.

But, as soon as she sat down, she saw her hands shivering. Her body felt uneasy. Strange even. It was then that she looked at those two girls.

In fact, she looked at every single girl in the class. Most of them were thin. Some were healthier. But, none of them was as heavily built as her.

And that's when she felt different. Even physically. Why was she made the way she was? Why wasn't she someone else?

Nine: Back in room

It had been nearly twenty minutes since she had returned to her room. The meteor shower had been beautiful. It felt weird describing things as beautiful.

She wondered what else was beautiful. Her mom. Her dad. Even Opa had been. Will someone else also ever describe her as beautiful? Even the thought tasted weird.

She turned her face and lay down sideways. The high neck sweater made her uncomfortable, so she removed it and tossed it aside.

It was weirdly warm for an October evening. But it had been cold outside. *Outside*. She didn't know if the meteor shower was still on, but she reasoned it must be.

They had decided to come back in after watching the spectacle for close to an hour. Her parents had seemed tired. They had had a long day, and she didn't want to keep them sitting outside because of her.

Now, however, she wanted to watch it some more.

She could slip into her balcony. Her parents wouldn't mind, would they? She was certain they would not. Moreover, they would be asleep by now.

Usually, slipping out into the balcony at midnight didn't count as an act of bravery. To Yaretzi though, it felt strangely brave because she'd never done it.

She stood on a chair and unbolted the door. A gush of cold wind touched her cheeks.

Why had she not done this before? Maybe, she had been lost in her thoughts or in something else. Or maybe, she just didn't listen to herself enough.

The stars were twinkling in the sky now. The meteors were still crossing each other - though farther and fewer in between.

There was a strange peace about the sky tonight. It was like the stars and the shooting meteors were creating their own symphony.

She liked being outside with them. She felt a deeper belonging with them than she'd felt anywhere else lately. It was then that she heard the loud howl. It came from somewhere outside.

It must be some animal she thought, and the howl returned. Slightly louder this time.

She gripped the railing bar with her hands and stood on her toes. All she could see was the front lawn and the endless black sky.

The howl came again. It seemed unnatural to her. Not something she'd ever heard in the area.

The howls began booming. They took over the winds, and when Yaretzi noticed, she realized that they were coming from opposite directions. Was it one animal or were there two? Could there be more?

She didn't want to be outside for longer. She was just through the balcony door – ready to go back in - when she heard the click.

On turning about, she saw a flash of green light in the sky. It was coming from somewhere above the roof shed.

Another clicking sound. And a red flash came on. The alternating howls were continuing. Immediately then, the sky was filled with the uproar of a metallic buzz. A loud vibration.

Yaretzi felt frozen in place. She could hear the beating of her heart even amidst those howls.

The door was just behind her. She could go back in, bolt the door shut and not think about it. Ever.

Or she could step closer to the railing and examine the source of these flashes and noise.

Most of the people in her place would have gone for the former. Or maybe gone back in and then thought about it. From a secure place.

Maybe she would have done the same on any given day. But, tonight seemed different. She had to find out what this commotion was all about.

A restlessness in her chest told her that if she went back in, she might never find out what this object was. *If* it was an object, at all. It would forever remain a mystery.

The howls were continuing but she couldn't hear them anymore. All she was focused at was the green and red flash.

And they say, you only ever need a few moments of astounding courage. Courage that pushes you to do things you wouldn't otherwise think of doing.

She walked forward and with her palm firmly gripping the railing bar, turned to look above the roof shed.

The commotion rose before dying altogether. Complete silence. And before Yaretzi could understand something, she found herself falling. Into what seemed like a deep abyss.

Ten: The after

She was jumping on the sofas once when she was just five or six.

That afternoon, only her grandfather was at home with her. Both her parents were at the restaurant. That had been their usual routine in Bougainvillea.

She had spent several afternoons with M. Soleil like that: just them together. That was the most time she had spent with any human being, if one came to think of that.

Their time together had given them several moments to talk with each other. Talk about anything. And everything.

Yaretzi told M. Soleil a lot of things. She called him Opa. There were many things that she told him which she'd not even shared with her parents.

Not that she planned for it to be this way. But, with Opa, there was just this connection that she felt. Words just flowed out easy.

It had been long since she felt this way with someone else. The words flowing out easy.

These days she even felt she'd developed an aversion towards talking. She just didn't know how to use words. What to say. How were some people so good with words? How could they so simply express what they felt?

That afternoon, while jumping, she had fallen off. Her grandfather had left his sudoku puzzle and come running.

The back of her head had hit the wooden leg of the sofa. It was painful.

She remembers herself crying. She couldn't control the tears. Maybe, she didn't even try to, at that age.

M. Soleil had sat down with her on the carpet and hugged her close. He kept pressing her head gently and saying, "It's okay. It'll be okay. I am there with you. You're not alone."

Those were the first words Yaretzi heard when she began to wake up.

Those words were all that she kept hearing for a while. Why did that memory return to her now? What was it trying to tell?

Her eyes were just half open, when she thought she saw sparks of colors.

They looked familiar. Their colors were bright. Or was it just bright light? She opened her eyes fully. The sun was shining.

She could feel its heat on her body. Beneath her was a barren land. There were cracks and dust for as far as her eyes could see.

She lifted herself using her elbows. Her body was aching. Even sitting up seemed hard.

Where was she? And what was this place? And the bigger question was: how did she get here?

She tried thinking back to the previous night and to the events that had taken place. She remembered the meteor shower. Even recalled stepping into the balcony. Those howls, those lights. She remembered falling.

And then - then what? The space in between was empty.

She focused hard to think and immediately then, their house from Bougainvillea filled her mind.

She felt odd standing outside the white fence. Behind it was a cover of grass, and in the corner, an orange tree. She'd plucked ripe fruits from it several times. Even tried climbing it once.

The branches of the tree weren't so high, and so, Opa had decided to follow her.

The climbing feat hadn't been successful for either of them. They'd received a few scratches along with scolding from David and Eiva.

In those days, it'd felt like Opa was her age. He never seemed old. Like he was a child who didn't grow old. Maybe, even refused to grow older.

When she reached the mahogany door, it opened itself and inside, she saw her younger self jumping on the sofas.

The same scene again. And then, she was left with the same words. "It's okay. It'll be okay. I am there with you. You're not alone."

When the scene and the voice left her, Yaretzi felt strangely at peace.

She felt a warmth in her body. She wasn't thinking about anything at that moment, just a feeling that told her it would all be okay. Somehow. And Yaretzi believed it.

The landscape before her, just then, began changing.

Eleven: The Meet

The dust and the cracks that she was seeing a while back, were replaced by grass. Fresh and succulent.

Amidst the grass, in scattered places, sprouted up flowers. Reds, blues, violets, pinks - in more hues than one can imagine.

Next in line were trees. Huge and solid. Their sprouting up sent a rumbling noise out in the land. Their trunks were thick and rusty brown, as though they'd been alive for many years and counting.

Right above, the sky had changed too. The scorching heat of the sun was replaced by the cool shade of clouds. Soft and white, like feathers. The sun seemed to be smiling from behind them.

A butterfly swept past her. It disappeared before Yaretzi could spot its colors, and then immediately after, a hundred or so butterflies emerged.

They circled the flowers before sitting down on them. She noticed their colors, this time. Orange and black with white spots. Monarch butterflies. She had heard stories about them.

What came next were rainbows. Tinier than she had ever seen them. They plopped between different clouds.

Their vibrancy touched the air, and a sweet scent followed. She knew this fragrance. It was the smell of those flowers. The white ones that had often fallen in her lap.

She turned around. There was a rustle of leaves and a rope fell out from one of the giant trees. And, on the rope came swinging a creature. One that she had not seen before.

There were many sounds the next moment. Boom, crash - a bang! The creature hit the ground. Yaretzi was wincing. It didn't seem like a smooth landing.

In that moment, she'd forgotten all fear or the fact that she must be cautious of this creature. All she wanted to know was if it - whatever it was - was okay.

The creature was lying with its face on the ground. Yaretzi couldn't decide if she should step forward and touch its back. How else would she know if it was okay?

She extended her hand towards it, and the creature suddenly jumped up and stood on its feet.

And that's when Yaretzi came face-to-face with a squirrel. Except, it looked nothing like any squirrel she had seen before.

The first thing that she noticed was its height. It reached almost the same level as her as she sat on the ground.

Then, it was blue in color. Deep blue. It had brown and black stripes on its bushy tail, and a body which was too big for his head.

The oddity of the whole situation was the familiarity in its eyes. They were a deep black with another circle of black fur around them. Why did she feel that she'd seen them before?

The creature extended its tiny palm towards her.

"Hi. My name is Ughets." (Pronounced You-ghet-eeze)

It put special emphasis on the last syllable, which revealed perfectly aligned white teeth. Yaretzi felt she even saw them shine.

There was no drama about the moment when she shook Ughets' hand. Nothing extraordinary.

There was no rapid beating of the heart, no nervousness and no weird sensation in the gut. And years later, when Yaretzi looked back to this moment, she realized its significance.

It was this that when we meet the things (people, situations or creatures) that are meant for us, there is no sense of unease.

Nothing feels out of place. There is no unrest in the body. What instead one experiences is alignment - in the body, heart and mind.

And it is from here that she learned how to gauge if something is meant for us. It's simple - it brings us joy.

She introduced herself and then the creature asked if she'd ever heard the story of acorns.

Yaretzi had not, so he offered to narrate it to her. She didn't know what other choice she had, so she agreed.

And that's how Ughets sat down next to her, on the bed of grass and shared one of his favorite stories.

Twelve: The story of Acorns

"Oak trees, that you see all around, grow from acorns. A single acorn – this tiny nut – can grow into a massive tree and start a huge forest.

Each acorn that is placed on the land, holds in it an infinite potential to become something bigger, something stronger, and something truly magnificent.

But, acorns even in their tiny form, do not question this magnificence. They do not wonder if another acorn is more suitable for becoming bigger, and not them. And they do not become harsh with themselves about not growing fast enough.

All they do is be themselves, and let the seasons do their magic. And as they go from one season to another, taking slow steps of growth, becoming more resilient in their being, they truly transform.

And one day, without even realizing, they become what they had set out to be: the mighty oak trees, spreading their branches in the forest.

But imagine, if tomorrow all acorns were to doubt this potential, if they were to question and ridicule themselves, how fewer oak trees would grace the planet, and how much beauty we'd miss witnessing."

Thirteen: Looking Around

Yaretzi loved stories.

She'd grown up listening to them. Opa and Yaretzi fed the birds, solved sudoku and gazed at the night-sky stars. What they also did, was to read out to each other different stories.

Opa had been an expert in storytelling. And on most occasions, he'd become the teller. Sometimes, he would just read out to her from a book.

This was another thing about Yaretzi's grandfather - he had loved collecting books. His study in Bougainvillea had had a huge bookshelf. And it was lined with books from bottom to top.

When he was not reading to her from a book, he would simply tell a tale from his memory.

Some of children, some of stars, and some of fields. He liked talking about these. He also liked talking about the universe and its mysteries.

Yaretzi had been much younger then and there were several times when she didn't understand what M. Soleil was talking about. But she still liked listening to him.

There was mystery and wonder in his stories. Maybe, that's what she liked listening to - the wonder and the mystery.

His eyes even lit up when he told those stories. Maybe, he'd liked telling them as much as she liked listening.

Ughets told her stories too and he took her around the place. It wasn't so big. The place where they had been sitting in was the garden of life, he'd said.

That was a peculiar name, Yaretzi thought. Why would they name something 'the garden of life?'

It was because, he said, it revolved between two extreme emotions. Almost like two different states of consciousness. Fear and love.

What one saw here was in direct correlation with what one experienced within.

If you experience fear, you will see something that matches that fear. On the other hand, if you experience love and ease, the landform will transform into something that matched that feeling.

So, there was no permanent face of the landscape in the garden of life, Ughets explained. It altered according to one's state of being.

The barren land and the beautiful garden - you saw what you experienced within.

When Yaretzi came here first, she was scared. Scared about the place unknown. And that's why what came before her was the barren land.

But when she began to feel at ease, the barren land and cracks disappeared. "They went away with your fears, Yaretzi."

She'd never heard of the outside being in direct correlation with the inside. And it led her to wonder what if one experienced the same elsewhere too - and not just in the garden of life.

What if our reality altered in accordance to the states we experienced? What would we do with such power? What reality would we create?

She wondered if she would then ever settle. If she would ever rest.

The next place her squirrel friend took her to, was where 'the beams' were situated.

Fourteen: The oldest boy

Monsieur Soleil had once talked to Yaretzi about his family. The one that he had had before he'd met her grandmother, and before her father was born.

Yaretzi had never got to meet her grandmother. She had passed away long before her birth - even before her parents had met in college. She'd never even seen a photo of hers. They didn't click them back then.

Opa, on several occasions, had told her though that she looked like her grandmother. She was the only one in the family who shared her blue eyes.

Before getting married, M. Soleil had lived in a village - the name of which Yaretzi could never remember.

But she could make from his descriptions that the village was small. Maybe, half the size of Bougainvillea. Or even smaller. She didn't know for sure, but that's how she remembered it.

He had five siblings - three sisters and two younger brothers. Two sisters were older - much older than M. Soleil had been, maybe at a difference of seven or eight years.

The third sister, Yaretzi couldn't recall, whether was older or younger. What she knew for sure was that Opa had been the oldest of the three brothers. He'd often described himself as the oldest boy of the household.

Maybe, that part had been tough for him. Being the oldest boy. Maybe, if he hadn't been the oldest boy, his life would have been different. Maybe. There was no way to know for sure.

Fifteen: The Beams

The walk from the garden of life, to the place of beams had been a long one.

Between these two, lay a big cover of white and blue. White clouds and the blue sky. The white clouds looked so delicate.

Yaretzi was apprehensive about stepping on them. She wasn't sure if they'd be able to carry her weight.

Ughets held her hand and told her to trust the clouds. It was weird hearing someone talk that way about inanimate objects.

But, she did. She trusted the clouds. What she didn't trust was herself. She didn't want to create damage, of any kind.

Under her first step, the clouds gave an appearance of melting.

The air from them - or was it the mist - rose and covered the upper part of her foot.

They were soft and bounced with each step that she took.

But, not for once did she feel that she would fall. Even with all that delicacy and softness, the clouds were firm.

Was there a reason behind this? She was sure there must be. Everything seemed to have reasons here. Their own story.

From a distance she saw the beams. They were made of colors and light. A lot of them.

It had been long since she'd run to chase an object. She'd run to catch falling kites, and to match flying birds. But that had been many years back. She hadn't done it in a while.

That moment though, when she saw the beams, she'd wanted to run.

Run at them and be near them as soon as she could. She wanted to touch them and feel their presence. Could she touch them? These beams. Whom did they belong to?

Panting, when she reached the entry point of this place, she couldn't see the blue sky anymore.

Above her, in front of her, and in fact everywhere she looked, were these beams of light. Millions of them. Or more. Yaretzi had never been good at the calculations.

When she stood in their midst, they crossed from above and behind her. They were all over the place. Scattered.

She couldn't see their starting and ending points. She didn't know where these beams had come from, and to where they were going.

Ughets had reached the entry point of this place too. Yaretzi gestured for him to come in. But he stopped there and did certain motions of the hand.

From that distance, he looked weird to her. She couldn't understand what he was doing. Sometimes - a lot of times - she didn't understand what he was doing. He did a lot of weird things. What did those gestures mean?

It looked like he had outspread his palms and was curling his fingers inwards. Like he was calling something towards himself.

He went on repeating the motions for some time, and then, she saw the transition occur.

The beams were shrinking. Their light and colors still intact.

They continued to shrink until she could see the blue sky between them, and further still until she could see the beams no more. Where had they gone?

She looked at Ughets, and above his palm, saw resting something cuboidal.

It looked like thin ice. When she went near it, she realized that the cuboid was transparent and within it lay all beams.

In their miniature form now, the beams looked like thin threads of a carpet. All in distinct colors.

When they were widespread in this place, they'd appeared random. As though somebody had just placed them here without a thought.

Inside the cuboid though, she had a bird's-eye view of them.

She could see here that the beams weren't just scattered but came together to form a detailed figure. Detailed and beautiful. Wow. She was again describing things as beautiful.

That made her smile.

She could keep looking at this shape, and at these threads. All of them seemed to hold a meaning. Like they had a part to play.

Ughets explained to her that what she was looking at was the miniature model of the universe. That sounded deep. Opa would have loved to hear about it.

"Each thread that you see here Yaretzi, each beam, represents a universal creation. To understand it better, you can think of it in terms of human life. Each beam here represents a life."

Ughets gestured for her to take a better look and see how these beams were deeply connected. And that's what she saw.

At different points, these beams touched one another and went on in newer directions. They formed a crisscross pattern when they did so.

What she also noticed was that at each point of this connection, at each meeting point, the colors of these beams seemed to diffuse into each other.

"Each beam in this model is significant. So much so, that if we were to remove even a single beam, it would all change. The figure they come to form, and the path of all other beams, even if slightly but most definitely, gets altered."

"That's the value of each beam, Yaretzi." He continued. "Of each life. That without it, the universe wouldn't be the same."

Sixteen: An Impact

Yaretzi didn't understand that world, but she wanted to know more. Like she had wanted to know about Opa and what his life had been.

Besides telling her about his siblings and the village, he'd never told her much about anything else.

Not about his parents. Not about his hobbies - about what he had liked to do as a child. All this Yaretzi began to think about after his passing.

About what his life had contained before. Maybe, she had never thought of it this way, that M. Soleil had lived a life even before she had known him. She saw him as her Opa, and that's how she'd seen him always.

But, when he passed away, she began to think about the life that he had left behind.

And the more she thought of it, the more she realized how less she knew of it.

She wished she could ask him some questions. Talk with him some more. Know a little more about his life.

Thoughts like these caused Yaretzi to think about her own life. About the part that she had already lived, and about the part that was left to come ahead.

Was there an impact that she was creating? Would she be remembered after she was gone away?

She had a habit of maintaining a diary. She had started writing it after seeing her mother. What started as an act of imitating her mom, had become her own source of respite.

Several times she flipped through the pages of her diaries at random. She never stopped at one page, and never reread it. It made her cringe, going through what she had written as a child.

But what she liked doing was being in the presence of those diaries; of flipping through them.

Because what they brought along was the remembrance of the time she had already lived. She could never judge if it was good or bad, or if good and bad were the only adjectives to even describe it.

But she had lived a life, and she hoped she had made an impact. Did she make an impact? Who decides that?

She looked at the beams, once again. There was something magical about them. But she couldn't decide what. She could never decide what.

She was curious about them. So, she inquired more. She wanted to absorb all that Ughets could tell her about these beams.

"The meeting points are the places where two beams meet - which means where two lives touch one another. The beams affect each other in beautiful ways, Yaretzi."

"One of these, of course, is the direct effect, as you can see from the meeting points. Two lives, or two beams cross paths and touch each other directly, either by thoughts, words or actions."

"The second way, and the not-so-obvious one, is slightly different. Can you guess what that might be? How can two beams that have never met still affect each other?"

Yaretzi didn't even have to think. The answer was right there in her mind.

"With the help of a third beam?"

Ughets was surprised by her response. She had grown wiser.

"Yes. Exactly that. With the help of a third beam, or maybe a fifth or a hundredth. You see Yaretzi, when two beams meet, their colors diffuse, they receive something from each other. They get impacted."

"And when they go ahead from here and meet more beams - the count of which is endless - they touch them in some way."

"The impact that one beam creates on the second beam, isn't limited to that beam alone. It continues to each beam that this second beam goes on to touch, and which they then go on to touch subsequently. The ripples go a long way, you see."

She did, and that made her feel something.

"Does that mean," she asked, "that all of us are somehow connected?"

"Yes. It does." He said. "But all humans are not only connected to each other, they are also connected with each plant, each bird, each animal…"

Before he could finish, she said, "Everything that is on the planet?"

"Not just on the planet, everything that is in the universe." Wow, that indeed was deep.

Ughets went on. "When two beams meet, their colors diffuse, because a part of them mixes. When they go ahead, they continue to carry this mixed part with them."

"So," Yaretzi's voice came out, "we carry a part of each beam that touches us?"

"Yes. And each beam that we touch carries a part of us."

Maybe then, she did have an impact.

Seventeen: The Yellow Beam

After restoring the beams to their original position, Ughets had taken a special interest in the Yellow beam.

This time, he did a reverse motion of hands. He expanded his fingers outwards, like he was sending something away.

This caused the Yellow beam to magnify and expand.

It became bigger than the other flowing beams. But the expansion didn't stop there. The Yellow beam kept expanding until within it, Yaretzi could see a set of fleeting visuals.

Like scenes from a life, running at a rapid speed. It was difficult to spot who was in them or what was happening.

When the Yellow beam was large enough, Ughets held Yaretzi's hands, and asked her to focus her attention on this one scene from the set of visuals.

While Yaretzi continued to focus on that scene, Ughets repeated the same motion of hands. Expanding his fingers outwards. Like sending something away.

Yaretzi didn't know why they were doing this, but all that they'd done so far had borne results, and she wanted to continue dwelling in it. In learning and seeing more.

In a few tries, the one scene that she was focusing on, began to enlarge and magnify. It stopped before them like a big screen and it was in it that Yaretzi saw the following.

It was four in the morning when David left his house.

He was dressed in black from head to toe. The hoodie did little to bring him relief as the cold wind collided with his cheeks.

He usually took two complete rounds of the field. That morning he'd felt like taking only one. Didn't have the energy for another.

He had not been able to sleep well the previous night. There was no reason for it, however. Just that he came late from work and then found it hard to fall asleep.

He felt tired when he sat on the bench. His body felt like it was breaking. Maybe, he could take the day off. That might help him.

Everyone in the house was still asleep - Eiva, his father and Yaretzi.

He was usually the first to rise each morning. Except the days he wasn't jogging. It did well to take a break, sometimes.

When he reached home, he wanted to go straight upstairs and slump on his bed.

But then, he saw the ajar door of his father's room downstairs and thought of checking up on him.

The room was dark, so it took a while for his eyes to adjust, but when they did, he saw his father lying on the floor.

The first impulse was to check for his breath and pulse. His father was still alive. He rushed upstairs to inform Eiva.

He didn't know what to do alone. His mind had stopped working.

Was it the shock of the moment or was it the unpreparedness? He didn't know. Eiva called the ambulance. It was arriving in ten minutes.

Back in their father's room, they tried performing any know-hows that they could. But nothing seemed to be making much difference. Any difference.

The hospital team arrived, and David assisted in carrying his father's body out to the van. Carrying his father in those moments, he had a strange recollection.

A picture of him sitting on his father's shoulders flashed in his mind. They'd gone to several fairs like that. Just him and his father.

He used to fear heights back then. But when his father told him to sit on his shoulders, he did. He'd felt fearless with him, even in that fear.

David decided to go to the hospital alone. He wanted Eiva to stay back home for Yaretzi. Their daughter was still asleep.

The drive from their home to the hospital would take just about twenty minutes, but even that seemed too long. All the way, David held his father's cold hand, and thought back to his childhood. Back to the time that they'd spent together.

After his mother's passing, it had only been him and his father at home. That had been their life for many years, before David got married, and eventually had a child.

David had liked living with his father, all those years. And it was strange in those moments to be thinking about all that.

Now, when David thinks of that morning, he feels that perhaps a part of him had known. Maybe, it had known what was to come ahead. And maybe, it was preparing him to say goodbye.

The ambulance came to a sudden halt. The staff of the medical center took his father straight in for examination. David waited in the corridor, just outside his father's room of admission.

He paced up and down anxiously and sat on the placed seat. Got up, walked some more and sat down again. The doctors came out. They informed him that his father had suffered a cardiac arrest. They asked him to wait some more as they carried out further observations.

He called Eiva to inform her. He wished she was beside him then, so he could just rest his head on her shoulder and have a cry.

Everything was moving too fast for him. He felt a strange panic crawling up his chest. He did not know what would happen. He did not know what to do.

Hardly ten minutes had passed, and the doctors came out again. His father had passed away. David didn't quite register that. Didn't want to. He looked from one doctor to another, searching their face for answers.

One of the them, an elderly woman, stepped forward and gently held David's shaking hand - 'It will be okay, son.' He gave them a subtle nod of his head, told them that he understood when no part of him did.

He decided to sit down on the seat for a few moments and gather himself. The pieces in him were beginning to crumble. A lot that he hadn't expressed to his father came to the surface.

He thought of all the times that he'd caused his father to be hurt or upset. It's strange how the unsaid decides to make its way through, when the time to say it passes.

When he finally found the courage, David made his way into the hospital room his father had breathed his last in.

His feet felt heavy as he dragged them to the hospital bed. He looked down at his father's face and his closed eyelids. He wished to see life in them still.

Gently, he ran his hand down his father's head and forehead. Monsieur Soleil had liked being caressed that way. 'I am sorry dad, and I love you.'

That morning, David placed a silent kiss on his father's cheek as a tear rolled down his own.

Eighteen: The Layers

The Yellow beam, thus realized Yaretzi, was the flowing stream of her father's consciousness, and that enlarged scene was a moment from his current life, a piece from time.

She had just finished watching the scene when she thought she saw those five sparkles again. Bright-colored and radiant.

They flashed for a moment and disappeared. Merging into thin air. She thought they might be a reflection from the beams. But, why had she seen them before?

Ughets restored the Yellow beam to its position and looked at her.

"Do you know why we saw that Yaretzi?"

He went on to explain. "It's because though a lot of moments have passed since that moment, your father still carries it within."

"He wonders if it was his fault in any way. If there was something he could have done. If he could have made it all okay."

"And when you go back, I want you to tell him that it wasn't his fault. It wasn't anybody's. That everything is still okay."

"That wherever your grandfather is, he is okay, and I am sure he would want your father to be okay too. Please, tell him all this, will you?"

Yaretzi nodded her head and thought, how there was so much about even her father that she didn't know.

How he was a book in himself, and how people carried so much within.

People had a lot of depth to them, she thought. They had a lot of layers. But she could never think the same about herself.

She could not see the depth and layers within herself. Did she also have them?

***

Yaretzi and Ughets returned to the garden of life, and there they just sat and talked.

The visual had stirred a lot of thoughts in Yaretzi's mind. It led her to think a lot. Something she did even otherwise.

That day, she thought about the morning at school. The first morning and how it had turned out for her. She hadn't talked about it with anybody yet.

She hadn't talked about it even with herself. And she didn't know the reasons. Why couldn't she get herself to talk about her feelings? Why did it seem so hard to even talk about them - to even just touch that topic?

And she knew not wanting to worry others was one aspect of it. She didn't want to put her load on somebody else.

But there was a deeper layer to it too. Another part of it. And it was because it felt stupid.

It felt silly to her what she had been feeling - and it felt sillier to even talk about it. Did other people also feel the same way?

Did they also feel silly about themselves and about what they had been feeling? Were we all fighting our own feelings and hiding them? Were we all just fighting our own selves?

Nineteen: The Name

Yaretzi was five years old when Eiva had come to her room one evening.

They seldom had those moments together - just the daughter and mom. David and Eiva's work at the hillside restaurant back then, had occupied a lot of their time.

That evening though, Eiva had something special in mind. She wanted to share with her daughter the story of her birth.

"That was a special day," Eiva recalled. It was raining, the day she got her labor pains. Everything had to be set up immediately.

Because of the weather outside - the possibility of a storm - and the sudden arrangements, none of the other family members could make it before the delivery.

It had just been Eiva, David, M. Soleil and their house in Bougainvillea, waiting for the new arrival.

Growing up, Eiva had seen the women in her family opt for water births and that is what she had in mind too.

In fact, when she had learned about her pregnancy, a water birth was the first thing that she had planned. Everything else she'd left on destiny to unfold.

"The rains were heavy," Eiva told Yaretzi. "I didn't know how it would all be managed. How things would turn out."

"The raindrops were splashing heavily on the window. It was even getting dark for the afternoon, but there was still a strange calm in the room. Maybe, it was the scented candles."

The room where Eiva had given birth to Yaretzi was lined with scented candles. The nurses must've placed them there.

They, along with David, had rubbed Eiva's back and brow constantly as she'd sat in that huge white tub. The gentle rubs and the warm water had helped much to soothe her pains.

"The physical pain that I was experiencing that morning was intense - something I'd rather not talk about." She said laughing.

"But even with that pain, I was happy inside." She looked in her daughter's eyes. "Happy that I would finally get to see you." Yaretzi was curled up next to her mother while listening to the story.

Along the months of pregnancy, both David and Eiva had looked through several names - some for boys, some for girls, some even gender neutral. They'd opted not to know the gender of the baby.

Eiva had liked none of the names that they'd come across. "No one name had seemed just right." She explained.

"It was in the final moments of the delivery though that I felt a warmth in my body."

"I remember that moment distinctly - as though everything happened in slow motion. You were out of me and the nurses had laid you on my chest."

"You were so small and so beautiful. I was looking at you, at your blue eyes. And then, this name came to me - out of nowhere almost. 'Yaretzi'."

"Looking at you, it just felt right."

"I still don't know how the name came to me that day. Maybe, I had heard it somewhere long back and then forgotten about it."

This was the only possible explanation Eiva could come up with. She didn't know how that name had come to her, or how she'd come to the name.

"Then you were with us, and we got into looking after you. Being parents for the first time, trust me, there were so many things we didn't know."

She was stroking her daughter's hair as she was recalling all this.

Yaretzi remembers feeling happy in her mother's presence that evening.

There was something about her mother's smile, about the way she had calmly told the story that made Yaretzi feel safe. She could sit with her mother that way, forever.

There was this charm that her mother carried. She gave away pleasant feelings like it came naturally to her. She even smiled at strangers.

Yaretzi couldn't do that. She couldn't even properly smile at the people she knew.

Sometimes, while growing up, Yaretzi thought about these moments - in which it was just her mother and she together.

They were rare then, these moments, but they were always special.

Yaretzi doesn't remember the latter part of the story. She didn't know how it ended - what else her mother had told.

All she remembers is that there was a knock on the door, and her father had come in.

He was informing her mother about a phone call downstairs. Her mother had left the room, and then later in the evening, both her parents had left for the restaurant. There was something urgent that had come up.

She'd slept in Opa's room after they'd left. That's all Yaretzi remembers of that evening.

Now though, thinking about it, she wondered if there was something more to the story.

If her mother had got to complete it that evening, or whether the story was left incomplete. And it was strange, that after all these years, she was thinking about that evening suddenly.

They were special, those moments and she could always have more of them. And sometimes, Yaretzi wished she was more like her mother.

Twenty: The Waterfall

There was a sound of water as they were walking. A splash. Yaretzi wanted to go and explore. But she could not see the water anywhere.

The sound of water splashing didn't die though, it only grew stronger with each forward step that they were taking.

A blanket of fog stood before them suddenly. Yaretzi didn't know if she could go in, if it was safe to go in, but she wanted to - because she could hear the water from the other side.

She looked at Ughets. He knew what she was thinking. "Look for it to find it." He said. And she stepped in. Immediately then, she heard a gurgling sound and she was transported to the land of bliss.

There was a high waterfall in front of her, that fell into a beautiful lake. The water was blue. And all around it were trees, plants and different grasses. The grass. That was beneath her feet too. The whole place was a mix of blue and green, and it was as peaceful as Yaretzi had felt in a long time.

Ughets asked her to kneel with him beside the lake and look in it. It was in its reflection that Yaretzi saw Master Jamie.

Master Jamie was a young boy - of about five or six - who was sitting that morning in a hall packed with students.

He was seated on the last seat of the first row and was holding on to a piece of paper quite nervously.

It was by looking at the whole arrangement and the incidents that followed, that Yaretzi understood that the visual was from a speech contest in a school.

All the participants were getting up on the stage one by one, and Jamie being the youngest, was the last to go on.

Different students talked about different topics - from music to the change that they would like to witness in the world. A younger student spoke about her fascination with candies and it was then Jamie's turn to go up.

The walk, from where he was seated to the stage, seemed like a long one, and Yaretzi could see how he kept holding onto that piece of paper in his hand.

Just before stepping in front of the mic, he shoved the paper in his pocket and began.

A volunteer jumped up to the stage and adjusted the mic stand's height. It was now right in front of Jamie's face.

That morning, Jamie talked about his family. About his uncle and aunt, and cousin Rhea. He talked about how he loved spending time with them, and why he felt family was important.

This is what he said.

"Good morning everyone. I am Jamie. Jamie McKay. And I am six years old. Today, I will be talking about 'my family.'"

Jamie's voice was weak, but firm, and Yaretzi could see his hands shaking.

"I chose this topic today, because family is important. Very. Family means people who support us, who care for us, and who love us a lot."

Jamie paused and repeated the last line. 'Family means people who support us, who care for us, and who love us a lot.'

And there was a pause again. Some teachers from the wings gestured to let him know that he could draw out the paper from his pocket and read from it.

Some students in the audience even clapped, trying to encourage Jamie to go on.

But it seemed to Yaretzi that Jamie wasn't noticing any of that. That he was unable to. All he did was stand there. Very quiet and visibly shaking.

Just then, as abruptly as he had paused, Jamie resumed speaking.

"When we are with people who look after us, and stand by us, every day feels beautiful and easy. I live with my uncle and aunt, and cousin Rhea. I like playing with Rhea because she is younger than me and whenever I go home, she hugs me. I like receiving hugs from her. They feel very warm and comfortable. What I also like about my family is that we always sit and have dinner together. We talk about how our day was and laugh a lot. That is always the favorite part of my day. And so, I wish that everyone in the world has three things."

He was pointing three fingers at the audience.

"One, hugs from the people they love and who love them. Two, people they can eat dinner with, and laugh, and talk about how their days went. And three, a lot of good memories, so that even if our loved ones are far away, we can look at the memories and remember them."

Jamie concluded by taking a bow. The audience members rose in an applause for him and Jamie smiled from ear to ear. He'd finally made it!

But, amongst everything that had taken place, Yaretzi had also noticed something else. Something that Ughets had wanted her to notice all through.

While Jamie had taken that long pause because he had forgotten a part of his speech, a white light had descended behind him.

It seemed to Yaretzi that it came from the ceiling of the stage, and then, just in the center of the white light two figures had appeared: a woman and a man.

The figures had both stood with a hand on Jamie's either shoulder and continued standing that way as he recalled and spoke out the remaining part of his speech.

"Those were his parents." Ughets told Yaretzi later. "They had both passed away, when Jamie was just one. But ever since then, they continue being there for him this way."

"Does Jamie know about this? About his parents being there?", she couldn't help but ask.

"Maybe he knows of it figuratively, but not literally. Maybe he just knows it from his heart. But, either way, they won't stop being there for him, and that's all that counts."

Twenty-One: Loved ones

Yaretzi's bond with M. Soleil was special. That went without saying.

He had been her best friend and most favorite ally for as long as she could remember.

And when he passed away, it felt to her that the world she'd known had stopped existing. If someone were to ask her to describe that feeling, she would not be able to.

She didn't know how to describe the loss of the only place of solace that you knew.

It wasn't just special, her bond with him. She knew it was rare. Those were the only two words she knew to describe it.

For many nights after her grandfather's passing, Yaretzi dreamt about him.

They were scary, those dreams. It felt like someone was snatching him from her. Like someone didn't want them to be together.

It'd felt unsafe and uncomfortable. And after a few months, she had stopped feeling much. Like she was growing numb. Not just to her grandfather, but to everything.

Maybe, there was so much to feel, that her mind was shutting off. Or maybe, she was just tired of feeling. She could never decide what was causing all those changes in her, just this that she was feeling empty.

Yes, that was the word. Empty. If a feeling like that did exist.

***

At the lake that day, Ughets showed Yaretzi two more visuals after that of Master Jamie.

In the first visual, Yaretzi saw a young girl bent over her bed, and trying to tie her shoelaces.

That was Maya, getting ready for school.

As Maya struggled with the shoelaces, Yaretzi saw a pink glow of light enter her room, and a slightly older girl flow in its middle.

The new girl had similar features and the exact shade of brown in the hair. And it didn't take Yaretzi long to figure that this was Maya's older sister.

In the moments that followed, Yaretzi saw how the new girl helped Maya, first to tie the shoelaces and then to pack her bag.

She sat down next to her sister and guided her hand movements. This caused Maya's shoelaces to be tied and glee to spread over her face.

The new girl then floated in the room and got out the study material from deep under various piles. She did all this while Maya read her class schedule for the day and got her bag out to get it ready for packing.

One by one, the new girl drew out the required books, and placed them in different spots in the room, where Maya could spot them easily.

As Maya finished packing her bag, and rushed out of her room, Yaretzi saw the elder girl smile to herself, and slowly disappear from the room - probably returning to wherever it was that she had come from.

In the third and the final visual at the lake that day, Yaretzi saw an old lady with five or six children seated around her. All of them looked thin and bony.

Yaretzi could see that the lady was very old, and her skin was wrinkled and folded in all places. Her hair was tied in a bun and the gown that she was wearing was too loose for her body.

The house looked old too. The wallpaper was torn and there was water dripping from the rooftop in many places. Their condition to Yaretzi didn't seem all that good.

What the old lady and the children were doing was attempting to watch television. Attempting, because the old lady was evidently struggling to get the T.V. switched on.

The children were staring at the small black screen. It was one of those old T.V.s with a thick and huge outer box, and a tiny screen. It was obvious from their faces how excited they were to see it come alive.

When it did not turn on even after pressing the remote button several times, she gave up and said to the children,

"Only your grandpa knew his way with this T.V. Only he could make this thing work. I don't know what he did or how he tried, but he could surely make it work. I am sorry I still haven't been able to figure my way with this."

She looked disappointed and lost. The kids though, came and hugged her instantly.

They told her it was okay and that she didn't have to be sad, because watching T.V. wasn't all that important. They would do something else.

'Maybe play outside,' one of them suggested. But they knew they wouldn't be able to do so, because it was raining outside. Heavily.

In their chitter-chatter, they didn't realize that a song had begun playing in the background and that the T.V. screen had come on.

When they did notice the new sound though, they were cheerfully clapping their hands. It was like their happiness knew no bounds. Even Yaretzi felt happy just by looking at them.

And then she saw above at the ceiling, a golden light was pouring through.

An old man was in its midst, with equally wrinkled and folded skin, and he was smiling as he looked at his wife and grandchildren.

He blew out, and bright sparkles of golden light left his fingertips and surrounded them all. The old lady looked up, smiled and whispered, "Thank you."

Maybe, she felt his presence, or maybe, she had a belief.

***

"Believe it or not Yaretzi," Ughets said later, "our loved ones are always there. They are looking after us in more ways than we can imagine, and they continue to love us even after they seem to be gone."

"All we have to do is call out to them - open ourselves to their presence, and we will find that they are there."

Was Opa looking out for her too? That was the first thing that came to her mind when she heard Ughets explain the visuals.

She wanted an answer to it, but it seemed too personal a question to ask Ughets. To ask anybody. So, she didn't. But she kept thinking about it.

Was Opa there? But she didn't call out for him. She never asked him to come. She never talked to him. She never knew if she could. She only thought of him in her head. Only kept him to herself.

The question kept returning to her - should she have called out for him? So, she asked Ughets.

"What if, we forget to call our loved ones? What if we don't ask out for them? Do they still look out for us?"

Ughets smiled at her and looked in her eyes. His own black were shining. "You may forget to call out to them, but you see Yaretzi, they will never forget to love you."

Opa was looking out for her, then she knew. But where was he?

Twenty-Two: The Second Tenet

Monsieur Soleil had once told Yaretzi about his childhood.

He'd rarely talked about that - about how his life was when he was a child. During that conversation, the only one they'd ever had, he told her about the field.

He said he'd started working there from a very young age. He had to earn to support his family.

And then, much later in his teens, when the field was sold off, he took up tailoring. He remained a tailor by profession until he stopped working - much later in his forties.

He didn't tell Yaretzi any further. They just never talked about it. But, sometimes after his passing she wondered if that was all he'd ever wanted to be. Or if he'd wanted to be someone else.

***

After they'd been to the beams and the waterfall, Ughets took her hands in his. He wanted to show her something else.

He'd said, he wanted to show her something from her memory. Yaretzi closed her eyes when he'd told her to, and immediately then, there was a visual in her mind.

It was raining and a dog was sitting on the street. A part of his skull, just near the ear, was bleeding.

There was a pool of water collected before him. The dog desperately tried to dip the affected area in it.

When that didn't help, he licked his paw and pressed it on his head. Whenever he removed his paw, the red part under it still shone clearly.

There was a girl standing and watching this dog. She was just four houses away from where he was sitting.

As she grabbed the iron bars of the main gate, Yaretzi saw the helplessness reflect in her eyes. It was clear that she wanted to do something for the dog. Just help him anyhow.

She was about to step out from her house, when a voice called from inside, "Where are you going? The rain is so heavy outside. Come back in."

So, she obeyed, but Yaretzi felt that the girl kept looking at the dog.

The scene remained stagnant for a few moments, with the dog still sitting outside in the dripping rain, and the girl looking at him from inside the gate.

Suddenly, the visual started running fast - like somebody had played a fast-forward button. It stopped at the scene when the sky was clear. The rain had stopped pouring outside.

Yaretzi saw the girl coming out of the front gate with a bowl in her hand. She walked up to the dog and placed the bowl before him. He looked at her suspiciously.

He sniffed the bowl once, and then dipped his face in it to begin eating. It was evident that he'd been hungry.

The girl wanted to pat the dog but thought otherwise, and leaving the dog with his bowl of food, she went back inside.

This visual collapsed, and the second visual sprang before Yaretzi as seamlessly as the first one had started.

This new visual contained a man walking in a park. He was wearing a white kurta-pajama and the sun was shining - almost creating a halo behind his head.

This old man was watering the plants as he was walking on the footpath.

A younger man stopped him and asked, "Why do you do this, sir? These aren't your home plants. You need not tend to them."

The old man smiled at him and said, "Plants are plants - whether at home or elsewhere." And he continued walking, peacefully doing what he did every day.

The third visual was of a girl in a café. She had brown splashes all over the apron that she was wearing. Coffee massacre, it seemed like.

She was attending the customers who walked up to the counter. The visual started with her talking to a couple who was travelling and had just stopped by for a quick bite.

She liked talking to people, this girl. It was evident from the way she smiled at them and tried to make conversations.

Suddenly, a grumpy looking man entered the café. He ignored the girl's question of how he was doing, just ordered item number 56, and went and sat on a corner table.

The girl seemed surprised by his behavior. Maybe, she wasn't used to customers acting this way.

The man, upon sitting, opened his briefcase and drew out from it an envelope. He tore it open and held two stapled sheets in his hand.

The girl, from behind the counter, observed him as she prepared his order. She saw his hands shaking.

When she walked up to him with the order, the man unaware raised his right arm suddenly. It collided with the order tray and the coffee spilled all over the table and his trousers.

It all happened so fast that it took a moment for the girl to register. She began at once to draw out napkins from her apron pocket.

The man got up and shouted at her, "What do you think you're doing? Can't you serve a drink properly?" He packed his briefcase hastily and began to leave.

The girl ran to and from the counter and got a packed sandwich and coffee case. "Sir, this is for you." She handed it to him, just as he was about to make his exit.

And then she added, almost as an afterthought, "Don't worry sir. Sooner or later, it all gets okay."

Yaretzi didn't understand why the girl chose to do so, and so Ughets asked her to look at the visual again, carefully.

It was then that she noticed that in all the chaos, the girl in the apron had read the title of the sheet that the man was reading from.

'Termination letter,' it had said, and that's why she chose to do what she did.

The fourth visual was of a boy in a packed bookstore. He had headphones stuck around his neck. That was the first thing Yaretzi noticed about him.

He was walking from aisle to aisle, looking through different bookshelves. He didn't touch any book or draw them out. Just looked at them from a distance.

Finally, he reached the last bookshelf and the visual narrowed down on a book. 'Alchemy: The art of turning everything into love,' it read.

"Yippie!" The boy screamed. The people around him stared at him for a moment.

He covered his head with the hoodie, and taking the book out, in a lowered voice said, "Finally found you."

He held the book close to his chest and smelled through its pages. There was a romance in that moment - between the boy and the book, and Yaretzi could see him smiling.

The last and fifth visual was of a woman. She must be in her mid-thirties, Yaretzi thought. The woman was wearing a thin coat and was walking along the pedestrian path.

She looked at the sun frequently and smiled as the sunshine touched her face. She also stopped ever so often and smelled any flower that came on the way. She took her time to touch the petals of these flowers and to take in their smell.

Everything suddenly became dark, and Yaretzi opened her eyes.

The visuals were over and Ughets wanted to know if she noticed something common in each of them. She did. She noticed a golden light.

When the girl placed the bowl of food before the dog, when the old man smiled and watered the plants, when the girl from the café handed that man a packed sandwich and coffee case.

When the boy with the headphones hugged his favorite book and when the lady smelled those flowers. Each time these events took place, a golden light came from the skies and surrounded them.

"It was the universe sending its love."

The golden light wasn't the only common aspect in all these events.

While explaining her about this light, Ughets also told her that all these moments had been drawn from Yaretzi's memory - which means, as they had taken place, Yaretzi had been present there too.

She and her parents were moving from Bougainvillea to the land of Iris, when they had crossed the little girl standing on her house's main gate and watching the injured dog.

At the age of six, she was taking a stroll in the park when she'd crossed that old man watering the plants.

That café was in Bougainvillea. And Yaretzi had been present in the market that day with her parents. It was the holiday season. They had walked by the man just as he was exiting the café.

She had been in the bookstore with M. Soleil when the boy had shouted from another aisle, and she was returning from her school once in Bougainvillea when she had crossed that lady.

Even though she didn't remember them consciously, Yaretzi had been a spectator - she had absorbed all these memories.

"This was to teach you the second tenet of the land." Ughets said.

"What was the first one?" Yaretzi asked.

"Oh! Did I not tell you about the first tenet?" He was forgetful like that. "I was supposed to share it with you in the garden of life."

He took out a long scroll from his sling bag. It was made of feathers. Feathers of different colors and sizes, the smallest one being as big as Ughets' finger.

He cleared his throat and read, "The first tenet of the land is, 'When in fear, think of love. When fear in us gives way to love, what we are looking at begins changing and the whole landscape transforms.'"

She could relate the first tenet to what she had learned at the garden of life. She remembered the whole incident of the barren land transforming into the colorful garden.

"What about the second tenet?" She asked.

"The second tenet, Yaretzi, the one that the visuals were here to teach you about is - 'When we take care of one of the universe's creations, the universe takes care of us.'"

She thought about it but couldn't quite relate it with all five visuals. "Whom," she asked confused, "were the people in the last two visuals taking care of? That boy in the bookstore and that lady walking on the pedestrian path?"

Ughets smiled, knowing much that this question would come. And then he answered, "Themselves."

And Yaretzi thought, she saw those five sparks again.

Twenty-Three: Sponges

It was an autumn morning when Mr. Brian had walked in the classroom. This was August - somewhere along the late weeks of Yaretzi's first month at school.

Outside, the leaves had crisped and begun to fall. The winds too were colder than they had been previously.

When he walked in, Yaretzi could notice the same spring in his steps - he'd found a new reading material to share with the class, for sure.

He wished the students 'good morning' and came back to him a singing reply, "Goooooood Morninnnngg, Mr. Brian." Yes, the singing continued still.

As soon as he'd finished taking the roll call, Mr. Brian started with what he had described as a 'gripping lesson.'

He placed his auburn briefcase on the teacher's desk, and out from it, drew a book. Books rarely do seem ordinary, but the one Mr. Brian had drawn out seemed exceptional.

None of the students had ever come across such a thick book, and never one with such black and golden binding.

The book probably had a thousand pages or more, Yaretzi guessed to herself.

When Mr. Brian removed the briefcase from sight, she got a proper view of the book. It didn't seem to carry any title. That was weird. What was he going to teach them about?

When Mr. Brian stopped flipping through the book's yellow pages, he placed it on his forearms and read from it. "Sponges."

There was deep satisfaction in his voice, and Yaretzi couldn't help but wonder if the professor didn't find the book too heavy.

He continued reading.

"Sponges fall under the phylum Porifera. All sponges are aquatic, mostly marine, solitary or colonial, sessile and they like warm water. Their body is porous and asymmetrical."

Then, he explained the terms that he'd just read out. Some of whose meanings are provided below:

PHYLUM is a category used in the classification of animal kingdom.

PORIFERA is the name of that category, or that phylum, to which sponges belong.

AQUATIC means relating to water, whereas MARINE means relating to sea.

SOLITARY means existing alone, and COLONIAL means living in groups, or colonies.

SESSILE is used to describe something, often a creature, that doesn't move.

POROUS means having small holes or pores, through which different materials can pass.

ASYMMETRICAL means something that doesn't have consistency or uniformity in shape. Sponges, specifically, come in a large variety of different shapes and sizes.

After the explanation, he read out some more.

"Sponges have openings around them and strong structures that are able to handle the high amounts of water that pass through them each day. They have been around a long time, this is because although the world is constantly changing, sponges are still able to respond to these changes through adapting to their environment."

He closed the book and kept it aside. Everybody thought the lesson was over, and so did Yaretzi.

But then, Mr. Brian said suddenly, "And some humans are like sponges."

It was as though there was a new awareness in the class suddenly. "Much like the sponges' pores, these humans have a sensitive layer around them, which causes them to absorb information from the outside."

"This layer allows them to take in other people's energy, thoughts and feelings."

In that moment, Yaretzi felt the teacher's gaze fall on her, though ever so lightly.

"I will now be describing a few traits of these human sponges." He went on. "They're often very sensitive, that is because they feel everything. They're also good listeners, that is because they can put themselves in the other person's shoes and feel exactly what they're feeling. If a friend or loved one of theirs is distraught, they begin feeling it too."

"They do not prefer being in crowds, and often need time alone or near nature, to charge their batteries."

"A human sponge is a wonderful thing to be, because it helps one connect with other people. To truly understand them, and to feel their emotions."

"But, there is a downside to it too, and it is this - if the sponges are not aware of this trait - of their capability to absorb other people's energy - what might also happen is that they can on certain occasions absorb information from the outside without actually knowing that they're doing so."

"Which means, that because of their outer sensitive layer, they might take in someone else's thoughts, emotions or feelings, and feel it in their body as their own."

A student from the front row asked if that was true - someone whose name Yaretzi still didn't know.

Mr. Brian smiled and replied that indeed it was. He went on to tell,

"This means that these human sponges might start to hold beliefs about themselves that weren't theirs to begin with. They were what someone else thought about them."

"And so, dear students," he concluded, "it would prove much a boon, if our beloved sponges understood this and realized that the opinions of others are best left where they'd sprung from: the outside."

"And in their heads, it's their own voice which must remain the strongest of all."

Twenty-Four: A conversation

The afternoon that they had sat in the garden of life, Ughets and Yaretzi had held a conversation.

Yaretzi was sleeping when she felt a weird texture on her body. She didn't realize when she had fallen asleep - maybe it was because of the long walk that they took to the place of beams.

When she got up, she saw a pile of leaves covering her. Many leaves - yellow, green and red. "What is it and who put it here?" the question escaped her mind.

"I did." Said Ughets. He was brushing his tail with a multi-colored comb.

"There was a loud noise from the sky, and the temperatures suddenly went down. I figured you would be cold." He spoke quite matter-of-factly.

Yaretzi thought to herself how different sometimes creatures turned out to be. Ughets, for example, had appeared like someone who was only concerned about his looks.

He carried a pair of black (mini) sunglasses and wore them often on his head. He didn't like to cover his eyes, he had said.

He also had a brown sling bag, from which he drew out many-many objects. After he had told Yaretzi the story of acorns, he had offered her those same nuts to eat.

He also had in the bag, speakers, cassettes and flashlight - when Yaretzi inquired about them, he said he didn't know how they had gotten inside his bag.

Now though, after spending the time with him that she did, she realized that he cared. He noticed even the small things. Some things which the other creatures might overlook.

He noticed, and he took care of them. Maybe, he just didn't like to show or talk about them. Maybe, he liked to keep his observations to himself.

A loud crackling sound brought Yaretzi back to this place.

"I think I just sat on the bag of nuts I had taken out." Ughets said in a goofy manner.

He was crazy, she thought. He was a crazy squirrel who liked to do crazy things. He too, sometimes seemed like a child.

"So, Yaretzi, I was thinking why don't we sit and talk today? You know, ask each other a few questions - maybe, get to know each other better? I would like to know you better."

That moment, Yaretzi thought she saw those five sparks again. Just in front of her eyes. They appeared and vanished the next moment.

She looked at Ughets, confused. "What happened?", he asked.

"Ah, nothing. Yea, we can talk." Talking wasn't something she was good at. But with Ughets, she thought, she could give it a try.

"Okay then Yaretzi, tell me something about your school."

"My school? What about it?"

"Anything you know - your likes, dislikes. Let's start with the simpler topic - What do you like about your school?"

"Umm, I like Ms. Smiths. She teaches us English. She is friendly and smiles a lot. It feels comfortable to ask her questions. I ask her questions a lot of times when the class gets over."

"Oh! This reminds me," Yaretzi went on, "Ms. Smiths had given us this home assignment once. A topic to write essay on. Can I ask you about that? I really liked that topic. I haven't been able to talk about that with anybody else."

"Sure. Go ahead."

"So, the question she gave us was: 'What is the bravest thing you have done?'"

"Hmm. That is an interesting question." Ughets noted.

He thought for a long time. Yaretzi wasn't even sure if he was going to give her an answer. What was he thinking about so deeply?

"You know Yaretzi," he said, "I am thinking about it, but nothing is coming to my mind just yet. Would you allow me some time? I will definitely get back to you with an answer."

So, he needed time. That was easy. She could give him time. It always helped to give people time if they needed that.

"So," he said, returning to where they had left off, "apart from your English teacher, what else do you like about school?"

"I like Mr. Brian's lessons. He teaches us Science. He always brings something interesting to the class. I like learning about the stuff that he shares with us."

"And," she went on, "the other thing that I like about my school is its trees. It has a lot of trees, and I like being around them."

"Oh! Even I like trees!" He said.

"I am sure you do, that's why you came swinging down from one, the first time we met."

He laughed. "No, the swinging down part was to surprise you." Then he became quiet suddenly, as though afraid of revealing too much.

He changed the topic to ask her, "So, you like trees, is that why you sit between those two trees every recess? Those two orange ones in the clearing?"

How did he know about the clearing?

But then, it came to her that he seemed to know a lot about a lot of things already, so where she sat in the clearing seemed like a small part of it.

"I just...sit in the clearing because I like it."

That was true. She liked being in the clearing. But that wasn't the entire part of it. She liked being in the clearing because she didn't like being in the classroom.

Or near a lot of her classmates. Or near a lot of people, in general.

And that began to happen after she heard Mia and Tessa's words. Their description of her on the first day of school.

Yaretzi had been unsure of herself many times, for many reasons: being fat hadn't been one of them. It didn't feel like a problem. It'd felt like a normal part of her. Had, for most of her life. That morning however, her classmates' words got ingrained in her.

She began looking at herself differently. She started looking at herself as though something was wrong with her, and she didn't know how to correct that.

And that's why she didn't feel like meeting people or talking to her classmates. She didn't want to learn about what they thought of her. If they also thought the same.

She just didn't want to deal with that. It didn't feel good.

She wanted to run away. Many times. And being away during the recess felt like her only option.

It felt secure among those trees. It felt okay to be there - without anyone judging her or looking at her as though something was wrong. It felt okay to be with herself, and alone.

That day, when Yaretzi sat with Ughets, she told him all of this.

It felt surprising to her that the words flowed easy. But it also felt relieving. Like something was taken off her chest.

And it felt good. She hadn't done this in a while - talking about what she felt. Talking about anything at all. But she still had her inhibitions.

She was mid-sentence when she suddenly stopped and asked Ughets, "I must be sounding silly, aren't I?"

"Why do you say that?" Ughets was displeased.

"Because," she was at a loss of words, "people my age are not supposed to have these problems."

Ughets didn't know who put that in her mind - what caused her to think that way.

He held both her hands in his and began talking. Yaretzi felt, he too was teary-eyed.

"I have met a lot of humans and they do this. They do this to themselves."

"They'll stop themselves mid-sentence because they think they sound silly or stupid or that no one would understand what they've got to say."

"Don't do this. Don't do this to yourself. It's okay to feel whatever you feel, and it is okay to talk about it. Whatever you feel," he looked in her eyes, "is okay."

And in a long time that afternoon, Yaretzi felt like something was okay.

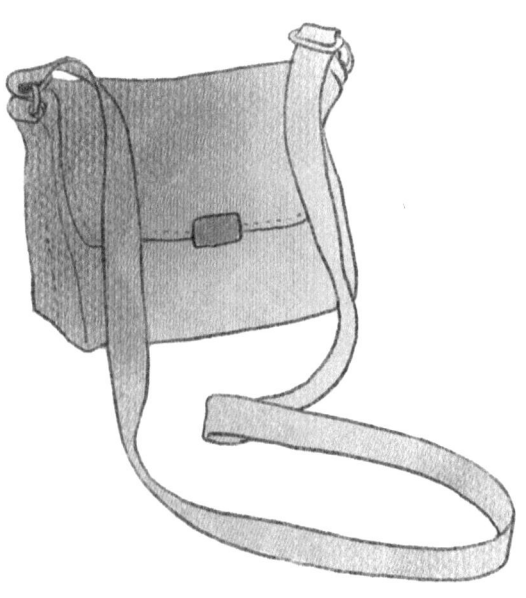

Ughets' Sling Bag

Twenty-Five: The Revelation

Being with Ughets was helping Yaretzi feel better about herself.

There was this energy beings carried - people and creatures - that made us feel a certain way about ourselves. Ughets' energy felt familiar, like Yaretzi had been with him before.

The ease didn't come eventually, it was there from the first moment that they'd met, and it travelled with them all through the time they spent together.

When Yaretzi had told him about what she had been experiencing, she'd also told him about her experiments to lose weight - how she'd examined herself every morning, and how she'd even tried to eat lesser food.

The latter part though, she had left soon because she was scared her parents might notice.

There was so much that Ughets wanted to tell her in that moment. So much that he wished to convey to this little girl.

Only one thing though came to his mind. He understood that Yaretzi had begun viewing herself from a different lens. And her classmates' words had done much to deepen that doubt in her.

They'd become this buffer between her and the world outside, and Yaretzi had forgotten how it felt like to be herself.

And it is this with words, the speaker might forget them, but with the listener, they can continue to linger for a long time.

So, during that conversation, Ughets came up with a plan.

He worked all night, and when Yaretzi awoke the next day, he took her for a walk along the garden of life.

Yaretzi liked being in this place - in the garden of life. She liked walking on the grass and watching the flowers and butterflies.

The landscape here had remained the same since the first time it changed. Yaretzi never saw the barren land there again.

It was while walking along the garden, that she took notice of a tree. Its trunk was thick and there was something hanging from each of its branches.

At first, she continued walking but then she thought of checking out the tree. When she came near, she saw that each branch had hung to it a chit.

She looked at Ughets, but he shrugged his shoulders. So, she opened the chit. 'Your long hair,' it read.

She opened another. 'Your blue eyes.' One more. 'Your love for blue pajamas.' And then, Yaretzi went in a circle around the whole tree, reading through each of those chits carefully.

'Your love for mushroom and caramelized shallot sandwiches.' 'The way you doodle.' 'The way you like reading books.' 'And listening to stories.'

'The way you got excited when you fed the swans and the geese.' 'Your enthusiasm to watch the night sky stars.' 'Your expertise in solving sudoku.' And Yaretzi stopped here.

She hadn't told about the sudoku incident to anybody else. Not even to her parents. It was just between her and…

When she looked behind, she didn't know if she was dreaming. She was looking at that five feet four inches tall man. The one with many wrinkles on his skin, and crescent shaped white hair on his head.

She was looking at those black eyes.

If she would have dreamt about this moment, if there was any way to prophesy it, Yaretzi would have imagined herself running. Running straight to hug her Opa.

But in that moment, she didn't run. Her body had stopped moving. Instead she felt herself crying. Heavily.

Like she had never cried before. Like all those emotions that she was carrying within herself had broken loose. She just sat down against the tree and cried.

She didn't stop when Monsieur Soleil stepped forward and embraced her in his arms. She didn't stop when he repeated to her those same words, "It's okay. You'll be okay. I am there with you. You're not alone."

Maybe, Opa had been there all along, but it was now that she did notice.

Twenty-Six: The Light Beings

It is this with people who have forgotten how to love themselves - there is this small thing about them - that they become vulnerable.

They become vulnerable for someone to remind them of who they were and of who they could be. But, mostly for someone to tell them of who they are already.

And for someone, who has forgotten these things about themselves, it helps if someone else can remember to remind them of their strengths.

And this is what Ughets did. The chits that he'd planted, contained the nuances - the little ways that made Yaretzi who she is.

And he wished that day that everybody got to feel that way about themselves - that they got to remember the things that made them unique, and deeply understand that there will never be another quite like them, again.

Monsieur Soleil let Yaretzi cry all she wanted to. It helped, he thought, to cry and release these emotions. When she finally sobered, he looked at her eyes and caressed her face.

This was his granddaughter.

It was difficult to describe what Yaretzi was feeling in that moment, though.

She didn't want to ask him anything, she didn't want to know how he got there. She just wanted to be with him in this embrace, while she could. It felt like she'd been home, after a long time.

"I want to show something to you." Monsieur Soleil whispered softly.

And then he looked up and said, "We are ready."

Just then, five bright sparkles appeared out of thin air, swept over Yaretzi and M. Soleil in a circle, and then stopped in the air, floating right above their heads. "Yaretzi, meet the light beings."

There was sudden recognition in Yaretzi's eyes. These were the five sparkles she had seen many times before - just never for long enough that she could fully register their presence.

The light beings were creatures of brilliant light. They were shaped like a stretched rhomboid, with the lower part of their body way longer than the upper.

They didn't have any human-like features. They had no arms, legs, eyes or ears. Not even a face. They were just light from top to bottom.

Their lights were all differently colored - Purple, Orange, Pink, Yellow and Green. As they stood together in an enclosed circle, their colors mixed with each other, and what reached M. Soleil and Yaretzi was a cumulative glow of their light.

"What the light beings do and are essentially is light. They are pure beings, full of light that lift the atmosphere around them."

"What you're seeing before you, are light beings in their true form. This is how they look when you see them for who they are - their light touches you, and you feel their warmth in your body."

"But light beings can take up different forms." M. Soleil went on. "The process of a long-lasting change is a little complex and requires certain conditions, so I won't get into it right now. But, sometimes on human grounds, light beings can temporarily change their forms."

"These temporary changes don't last for long, and in these, the light beings can't change their forms in entirety. But they can don a hand or a leg - temporarily - anything that allows them to get things done."

Looking at them in their true form, it seemed queer to Yaretzi to imagine them with a hand or leg.

Orange then, as though having sensed her mind, changed its shape that instant. The pointed corners on its side had disappeared, and in its place were two arms - much human-like but in the color of its remaining body. They had come out of it so naturally, as though they were always meant to be there.

The next moment, it went back to its original shape, and the arms disappeared.

She was amazed by the fluidity of the motion, and M. Soleil held her by the shoulders to say, "So, Yaretzi, this is my team and they helped me get you here."

He smiled at her and then, at the light beings.

Twenty-Seven: Behind the Scenes

M. Soleil liked to call the light beings by the colors they were. It made it easy for him to remember and refer to them.

Purple, Orange, Pink, Yellow and Green had become his team - the five light beings.

"So," he said, continuing the explanation, "our work together started on the day you received that poster. But, the story that I've to tell you goes slightly back."

"The thing is Yaretzi, even though I've been here, I have been looking out for you."

"Not just for you, but for your parents as well. Things with you were working okay, until well of course, you reached your new school."

The mentioning of school made her more aware suddenly. Yaretzi thought she knew what was coming, still not so much.

"I saw what happened there," her grandfather continued, "and I understood how it made you feel. I saw how you'd begun looking at yourself differently."

"My first take was that you would talk to your parents and it would get okay. That you would eventually feel alright."

"But days passed, and you didn't. You didn't talk to them or to anybody, and the incident kept bothering you. So, I knew I had to intervene."

"So, this is where our story officially unfolds." He clapped his hands and gave her a big smile. Still theatrical. And she knew her grandfather still liked to tell stories.

"The first thing I did was to come up with a list of books and movies for you to read and watch. Anything that would empower you, really." And Yaretzi immediately remembered the phase when her mind was filled with all these ideas.

About all these different books and movies. Sometimes - well, many times - she'd even questioned where she was getting all these ideas from. It did seem strange that her mind was suddenly birthing all these.

"They came from me." M. Soleil said. "Those ideas. They were my whispers."

"But that didn't work," he went on, "so I tried dropping a few of those books during your library lessons."

"I thought maybe if you saw the book dropping before you, it might pique your interest in it. But boy, I was wrong!"

He said laughing. "My dear granddaughter here, just picked them and placed them back in the shelf without reading. Even a bit."

"So, there was a plan three. That was to give your mother the suggestion of putting up some beautiful photos on the walls."

"Oh, so you told her to do it?" She asked.

"Well, not tell her exactly. Just gave her the whisper. Going ahead with it was her choice."

"Anyway, so this plan was to put up certain photos. Photos that represented memorable times of your life - that you could look at and maybe, feel the feeling you experienced when you were in them."

"But again, it was in vain." He shook his head. "You just used the staircase to run up and down. Never stood opposite those photos to watch them. Never looked at them for more than a few seconds." There was good humor in his voice.

"And ladies and gentlemen, thus, we had to come up with a master plan." Well, there were no ladies and gentlemen, but the theatrics continued.

"And the master plan was to call me here?" Yaretzi asked.

"Indeed, it was." He smiled with all his teeth.

"And it was here that the five light beings helped me. Well, they helped me in a lot of other things. But, this one dominantly."

As he talked about them, Yaretzi looked at the five light beings. They were still floating in a quiet circle around them.

She then closed her eyes and Monsieur Soleil put an image in her mind.

She saw the clearing of school, and herself seated here. With her knees hugged close to her chest. It was from the day she received the poster she knew almost instantly.

She remembered this afternoon and this moment. It was here that she had made a wish.

That day in school, she'd been missing Opa a lot, and she'd wished to be able to meet him once.

Looking at her grandfather before her then, she shuddered at the synchronicity of the moment, for it was this wish that had set the events rolling.

The visual continued, and Yaretzi saw Purple appear out of thin air. It appeared with both his human arms attached, and gently before her placed a white sheet of paper. The poster.

She saw how Purple first placed it face up, and then flipped it over to the backside.

"Well, all of us thought, that it would be better if you received the poster with its back facing up." Opa explained.

"Oh, so were you all there too?", she asked.

"Well, not technically. But yes, we were. The light beings do not need to be physically in the same plane to send messages."

That's when Monsieur Soleil explained the communication with light beings. Light beings don't communicate with us, or with each other, using voice or audible words.

"What they speak to us instead is in thoughts and feelings. That's how they drop us messages - by placing a certain block of thought in our heads, or by the feelings we feel in our body, particularly warmth and joy."

"And that is why, there is no physical parameter of distance between the light beings and humans. You don't need to see them to be able to communicate with them. The heart is from where their voice reaches us."

The visual rolled further, and Yaretzi saw the evening of the meteor shower.

"The meteor shower was put up with the help of the meteors. Yellow and Pink had gone up to them to communicate the plan."

She looked at Yellow and Pink, and felt their glow brighten.

The poster, and the meteor shower subsequently, were put up to grab Yaretzi's attention.

As M. Soleil explained, "To bring to you something which was different from the experiences that you were having. Something that would feel out of the ordinary."

And of course, the idea had a lot to do with the grandfather and granddaughter's collective fascination with watching the star-lit sky.

"It was a piece of you and me together." He said, "The stars and the night sky."

As the visual progressed, Yaretzi saw herself in the balcony. When she'd come out to watch the meteor shower some more. She also saw Orange and Purple floating right outside her home.

They were both in opposite corners and had in their hand, a cassette player each. (Which, they had procured, just moments ago, from a separate household).

"The thing with light beings is that although they are brilliant at what they do, they can at times get stuck with human inventions. And this is what had happened that night."

The task of playing the cassette was assigned to Orange alone. But Orange wasn't so sure if it would be able to pull the entire insert the cassette - press the play button once - and turn it off drill on its own.

"So, Purple had volunteered to be there too. With a separate cassette and cassette player in hand - you know just in case Orange's attempt went, well umm, a little haywire."

The cassettes had in them those howls recorded. The plan was to play the button only once and have a single howl come out, so to get Yaretzi curious.

"Everything was set, and Orange pressed the play button. No sound came out, so it tried again. When no sound came out even in the second try, Purple sent a signal to Orange to let it know that it would take it from there."

"So, Purple pressed the button and that is how you heard the first howl. It caught your attention and our job was done."

"Immediately then however, a howl came out from Orange's player. None of us knew how. Orange was frantic - because it had not pressed any buttons! So, Purple floated to its side to help it handle the cassette player. They were handling this one, when Purple's cassette player on the other side produced another howl."

"The remaining howls that you heard," he concluded, "were produced as Orange and Purple tried to handle each other's cassette player and that of their own."

Yaretzi saw in the visual how Purple and Orange were rushing from one side to the other.

It was hilarious to watch the confusion and chaos between them - but it was also endearing. It felt endearing to watch someone go to such lengths for her. And she felt gratitude that they did so. That they did so just so she could be here.

As the visual went further, she saw herself standing in the balcony, transfixed, as the other three light beings created what she saw as the red-green flashes and heard as the electric buzz in the sky.

Her grandfather explained, "The red and green flashlights and the electric buzz were also signs, to grab your attention. They were steppingstones to see if you'd step forward to explore the unknown."

"The flashes were meant to go on only once, but for some reason, Pink and Yellow developed a new fascination with the flashlights and decided to duel with them.

The electric buzz was created by Green - that was its collaboration with the winds."

Yaretzi was still looking at the visuals when she asked, "Opa, if you wanted me to come here, couldn't you just get me here?"

"Like how, you mean?"

"I don't know. Maybe, just picked me up from the balcony or my room or something. What I mean is - why did you have to go to such heights?"

"Well, of course, we wanted you to be here, but the answer to your question is no. We couldn't just pick you up from the balcony - or elsewhere. That had to come from you."

"You see Yaretzi, what we did was lay steppingstones. Stones that would lead to the unfolding of the path as it did."

"But, the choice to walk on those stones was yours. Everything from picking up the poster, to taking those final steps towards the railing to explore the source of the flashes and noise, was each a choice that you made."

"And so, it is with all in life. It is you - your choices and courage - that has the final say.

That determines how the path would unfold."

"When you made the final choice that night, you told us that you were ready to explore the unknown. And that's what led you here."

In the visuals then, she saw how when she'd fallen from the balcony, each of the five light beings had glided to her side.

They caught her mid-air, and gently carried her through the ethers. And she saw herself floating, as her body was immersed in their collective glow of light.

Twenty-Eight: The Bravest Thing

Yaretzi was absorbed in the story. Meeting Opa, the light beings, and understanding how everything had taken place was overwhelming.

Even though it made her happy to learn about it, she didn't know how to react - because there was just so much to take in. But there was one thing that kept returning to her, and it was this that they did all this for her. It was a different feeling - feeling loved.

***

"Before you go back," M. Soleil said, "there's another thing that I have to tell. Remember that evening you asked me this question - about the bravest thing I did."

"Well, I am going to tell you about the bravest thing I didn't do - I didn't listen to myself."

The words had just come out of Opa when before Yaretzi a visual appeared.

She saw a young boy lying on grass. As the scene zoomed out, she understood that what the boy was lying on, was a part of a large field.

There was a plough next to him - soiled and broken from the edges. The boy lay with his arms folded behind his head and was gazing at the stars. His eyes were black.

"Is that you, Opa?" Yaretzi asked as the visual disappeared.

"Yes." He said. "When I was little, I loved looking at stars. I loved it even when I was old."

"There was a fascination I felt with them, a pull. Something that would constantly call me towards itself."

Yaretzi was listening.

"I was eight when my mother came to me one afternoon. She didn't usually pick me up from school, but that afternoon she did.

And I knew it was a sign of something really good or *really* bad."

"She lifted me up, hugged me and then told me I would not be able to go to school anymore. My father had suffered a job loss, so they couldn't continue sending me there."

"And then she added, they needed more hands with the earnings, so I would have to step up, since I was the oldest boy of the household."

"My mother said I could wait a few days before starting, but I didn't. I was at Mr. Roger's field the next day."

"For the next nine odd years, I worked with Mr. Roger. I worked on his field. We ploughed, we sowed, we harvested. There was work through all seasons."

"Then, one evening suddenly, Mr. Roger decided to sell off the field and move away, and I was rendered jobless. A mate of mine told me about this new thing - a sewing machine that was doing the rounds in our village, and I went for that."

"That's how for the next thirty or so years, your grandfather worked as a tailor."

"In all those years, there was one thing I didn't tell anybody, Yaretzi, and it was this that I had wanted to be an astronomer."

"Why? Why didn't you talk about it?", she asked.

"It seemed silly," he said, "even improbable, from where I was looking at it anyway. So, I just kept it with me. The thought, the fascination, and the pull. I thought it would go away."

"But, that's the thing about it. This pull. It never does go away."

"And that's the answer to your question, Yaretzi. The bravest thing I could have done but didn't do. I didn't listen to this pull."

***

Yaretzi was quiet but decided to ask. A question that was bothering her all through. "Opa, where is Ughets?"

She hadn't seen him since he'd brought her to the garden of life.

"OH!" M. Soleil exclaimed. "I am silly, aren't I? How could I forget about this important thing!"

The light beings glowed brighter as though they too were agreeing.

M. Soleil clicked his fingers, and before Yaretzi then was sitting a squirrel. *The* squirrel.

The squirrel clicked his fingers and then before her was M. Soleil. It took a while for her to register, and then Opa said,

"Yes, I am Ughets and Ughets is me."

"Why didn't you meet me as yourself?", she asked.

"Well, because I wanted to meet you as a friend."

Twenty-Nine: The Final One

Yaretzi woke up and remembered faintly her last conversation with M. Soleil.

It was about a message he'd asked her to find. A message that was for her, he'd said. A message that had been there for her, always.

When she'd bugged him for clues, he'd finally given in to say nothing but a line, "It's in the name."

Just moments after she'd woken up, Eiva came to her room to ask if she'd slept on time after watching the meteor shower last night.

At first, Yaretzi didn't understand, and then she looked at her bedside table clock and calendar, which read, 'October thirtieth, Sunday.'

So, she'd only been away for a night, she thought to herself. But it seemed like a long time on the other side.

Eiva was drawing open the curtains of the room, all the while talking to Yaretzi. About breakfast that her dad was getting ready downstairs, and about how she'd like to spend her off day from school.

Even though Yaretzi was listening, her mind was elsewhere. She was thinking about 'the message.'

Suddenly though, in her head, entered an idea, speaking to her directly. And she asked her mom, out of the blue.

"Mum, did you finish telling me that story about my birth?"

"What?" The half-opened curtain was left hanging loose.

"That story. Remember back in Bougainvillea, you came to my room one evening and told me the story of my birth. But then dad came up and said there was a phone call for you downstairs. And then, both of you had to rush to the restaurant."

"Oh. Yea. I remember it slightly." There was faint recollection on Eiva's face.

"So? Do you remember if you got to finish the story? Was there anything else that you had thought to tell?"

"Well," her mother was sitting on her bed now, "I must've finished it. This was so long ago, I don't remember if, wait. WAIT!" Eiva's eyes were large suddenly. "Did I show you my diary?"

"What?"

"That evening - when I was telling you the story or later around that time, did I show you my diary?"

"Umm, I don't think so."

She rushed to her room and came back - this time with her diary. "So," she said, "I told you about your name, right? How it suddenly came to me when I held you for the first time?"

Yaretzi nodded her head.

"After your birth, it was after I think six-seven months or more, I realised that I didn't know the meaning of your name."

"That was a silly thought, but while naming you, we just went with the phonetics of it. And although, keeping names with meaning isn't such a norm, I wanted to know if your name had a meaning. And if it did, what it meant."

"And it's crazy, that all this while I have never told you that. You're thirteen, and I am sharing this with you now. Maybe, everything has its time." She shrugged her shoulders.

But Yaretzi knew this line wasn't hers.

"Anyway," Eiva continued, "I got out this book with a hundred or maybe more baby names. I flipped through it, and surely yours was there."

What she read in the book, Eiva had copied down word-to-word in her diary. She asked her daughter then, if she'd want to read it for herself.

Her daughter did, and this is what she read, "YARETZI is an AZTEC term which translates to, 'You will always be loved.'"

She looked up and saw her Opa and the five sparkles appear for a moment near her ceiling.

And she knew then this was 'the message' for her. Perhaps, it is for us too.

*****

Yaretzi and Ughets

About the Author

Kanika Marwah believes words to be potent portals that transform and heal. She believes in gold dust, magic and the sheer beauty of love and joy.

There is great power, she feels, in dancing to the rhythms of one's heart, and this is the simple philosophy she advocates and lives by. Currently, she lives in New Delhi, India with her parents, brother, sister and books, of course.

www.ingramcontent.com/pod-product-compliance
Lightning Source LLC
LaVergne TN
LVHW041839070526
838199LV00045BA/1356